Quantitative Reasoning

1

PEGASUS
www.pegasusforkids.com

Published by Kuldeep Jain for B. Jain Publishers (P) Ltd., D-157, Sector 63, Noida - 201307, U.P.
Registered office: 1921/10, Chuna Mandi, Paharganj, New Delhi-110055

Printed in India

CONTENTS

EXERCISE 1

NUMBERS 1-100

Let's read and learn:

1	11	21	31	41	51	61	71	81	91
2	12	22	32	42	52	62	72	82	92
3	13	23	33	43	53	63	73	83	93
4	14	24	34	44	54	64	74	84	94
5	15	25	35	45	55	65	75	85	95
6	16	26	36	46	56	66	76	86	96
7	17	27	37	47	57	67	77	87	97
8	18	28	38	48	58	68	78	88	98
9	19	29	39	49	59	69	79	89	99
10	20	30	40	50	60	70	80	90	100

Date.................. Remarks..................... Signature.....................

EXERCISE 2

MISSING NUMBERS

A. Write the missing numbers in the box:

1.	13	14		16		18		
2.		31				35		
3.			10					15
4.	46			49		51		
5.	75			78		80		82
6.		55		57			60	
7.			24		26		28	
8.		91			94		96	
9.	84				88		90	
10.			66			69		71

Date.................... Remarks.................... Signature....................

B. Write the backward counting:

1.	21	20	19			16		
2.	19		17		15		13	
3.	31			28	27		25	
4.			14		12	11		
5.	47		45				41	
6.	62					57		
7.	70		68		66			63
8.	100			97				93
9.	54				50			
10.	80				76		74	
11.		69				65		
12.			59		57			

Date.................... Remarks..................... Signature.....................

EXERCISE 3

NUMBERS 101–200

Let's read and learn:

101	111	121	131	141	151	161	171	181	191
102	112	122	132	142	152	162	172	182	192
103	113	123	133	143	153	163	173	183	193
104	114	124	134	144	154	164	174	184	194
105	115	125	135	145	155	165	175	185	195
106	116	126	136	146	156	166	176	186	196
107	117	127	137	147	157	167	177	187	197
108	118	128	138	148	158	168	178	188	198
109	119	129	139	149	159	169	179	189	199
110	120	130	140	150	160	170	180	190	200

Date.................... Remarks.................... Signature....................

EXERCISE 4

SKIP COUNTING

Let's learn and write:

1.	101			104	105			108		110
2.							117			120
3.		122	123						129	
4.				134			137	138		
5.		142			145	146				150
6.		152		154	155		157	158		160
7.	161			164			167		169	
8.	171		173			176			179	
9.	181		183				187			190
10.		192				196			199	

Date.................... Remarks..................... Signature.....................

EXERCISE 5
BACKWARD COUNTING

Count backwards and write the numbers:

1.		150		148		146
2.		144			141	140
3.		138	137			134
4.	133		131		129	
5.	127			124		
6.	121		119			116

Date.................. Remarks..................... Signature.....................

EXERCISE 6

MIXED NUMBERS

A. Write in order. Start from the smallest one:

EXAMPLE:

16, 15, 14, 17, 12, 13 = 12, 13, 14, 15, 16, 17

1. 24, 26, 23, 25, 22, 21 = 21, ___, ___, ___, ___, ___
2. 55, 58, 60, 57, 56, 59 = 55, ___, ___, ___, ___, ___
3. 18, 17, 16, 15, 13, 14 = 13, ___, ___, ___, ___, ___
4. 63, 67, 62, 66, 65, 64 = 62, ___, ___, ___, ___, ___
5. 48, 44, 47, 45, 46, 49 = 44, ___, ___, ___, ___, ___
6. 56, 58, 60, 57, 59, 61 = 56, ___, ___, ___, ___, ___
7. 29, 27, 31, 28, 32, 30 = 27, ___, ___, ___, ___, ___
8. 58, 62, 59, 63, 60, 61 = 58, ___, ___, ___, ___, ___
9. 77, 79, 76, 78, 75, 74 = 74, ___, ___, ___, ___, ___
10. 40, 43, 44, 39, 41, 42 = 39, ___, ___, ___, ___, ___

Date.................. Remarks.................... Signature....................

B. Write the numbers in order:

EXAMPLE:

44, 43, 42, 41, 40, 39 = 39, 40, 41, 42, 43, 44

1. 50, 49, 48, 47, 46, 45 = ___, ___, ___, ___, ___, ___
2. 38, 37, 36, 35, 34, 33 = ___, ___, ___, ___, ___, ___
3. 26, 25, 24, 23, 22, 21 = ___, ___, ___, ___, ___, ___
4. 19, 18, 17, 16, 15, 14 = ___, ___, ___, ___, ___, ___
5. 32, 31, 30, 29, 28, 27 = ___, ___, ___, ___, ___, ___
6. 38, 37, 36, 35, 34, 33 = ___, ___, ___, ___, ___, ___
7. 15, 14, 13, 12, 11, 10 = ___, ___, ___, ___, ___, ___
8. 30, 29, 28, 27, 26, 25 = ___, ___, ___, ___, ___, ___
9. 87, 86, 85, 84 83, 82 = ___, ___, ___, ___, ___, ___
10. 53, 52, 51, 50, 49, 48 = ___, ___, ___, ___, ___, ___
11. 79, 78, 77, 76, 75, 74 = ___, ___, ___, ___, ___, ___
12. 97, 96, 95, 94, 93, 92 = ___, ___, ___, ___, ___, ___

Date.................. Remarks.................... Signature....................

C. Practise more:

EXAMPLE:

143, 142, 141, 140, 139 = 139, 140, 141, 142, 143

1. 150, 149, 148, 147, 146 = ___, ___, ___, ___, ___,

2. 192, 191, 190,189, 188 = ___, ___, ___, ___, ___,

3. 129, 128, 127, 126, 125 = ___, ___, ___, ___, ___,

4. 187, 186, 185, 184 183 = ___, ___, ___, ___, ___,

5. 100, 99, 98, 97, 96 = ___, ___, ___, ___, ___,

6. 177, 176, 175, 174, 173 = ___, ___, ___, ___, ___,

7. 169, 168, 167, 166, 165 = ___, ___, ___, ___, ___,

8. 136, 135, 134, 133, 132 = ___, ___, ___, ___, ___,

9. 114, 113, 112, 111, 110 = ___, ___, ___, ___, ___,

10. 129, 128, 127, 126, 125 = ___, ___, ___, ___, ___,

11. 186, 185, 184 183, 182 = ___, ___, ___, ___, ___,

12. 126, 125, 124, 123, 122 = ___, ___, ___, ___, ___,

Date.................. Remarks.................... Signature....................

EXERCISE 7
ASCENDING ORDER

A. Write the numbers in ascending order:

EXAMPLE:

1.

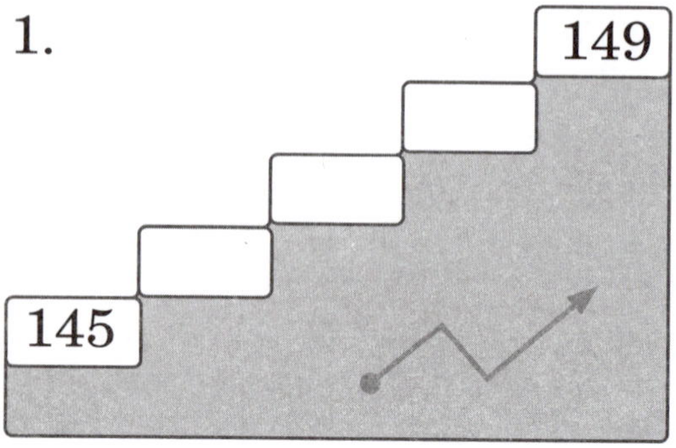

2.

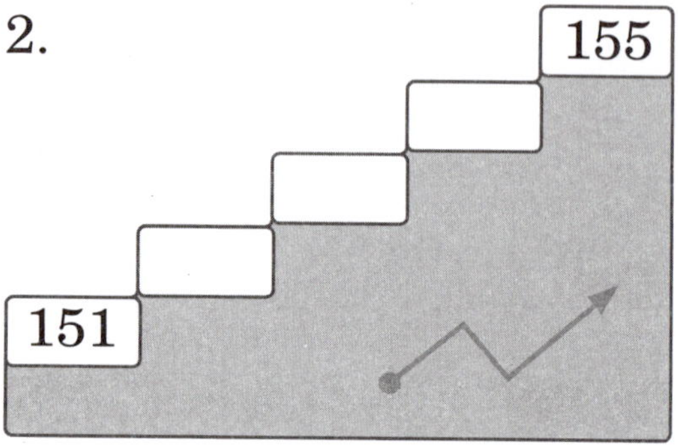

3.

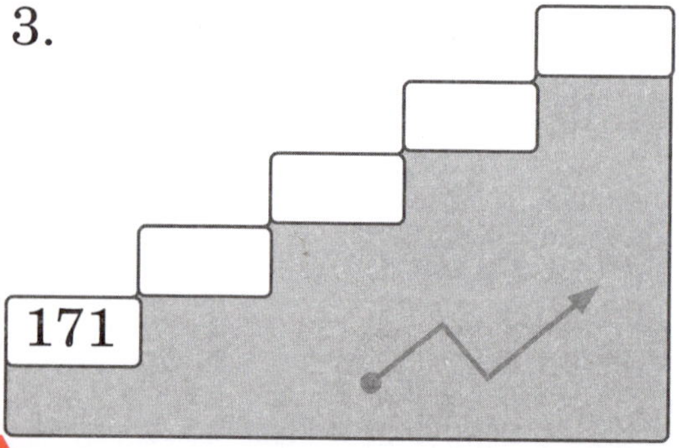

4.

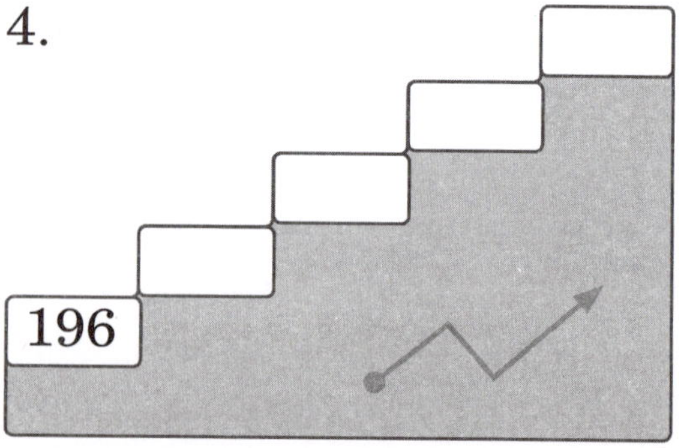

Date.................... Remarks..................... Signature.....................

5.

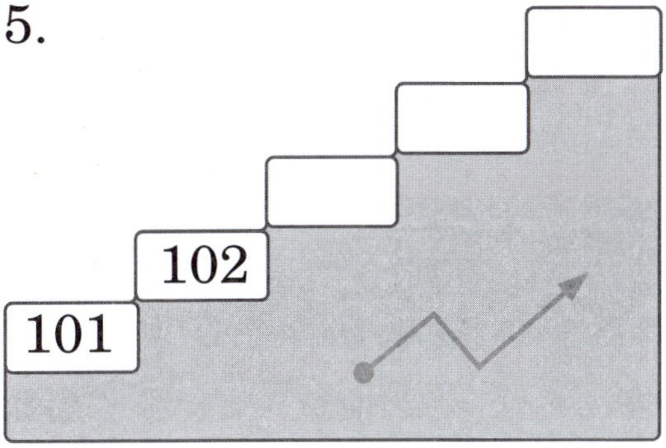

6.

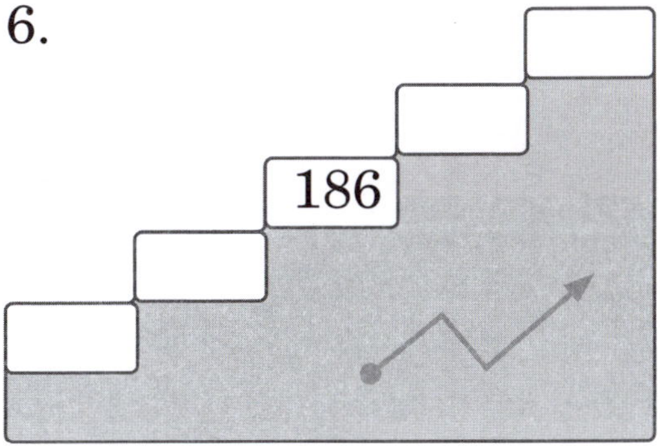

7.

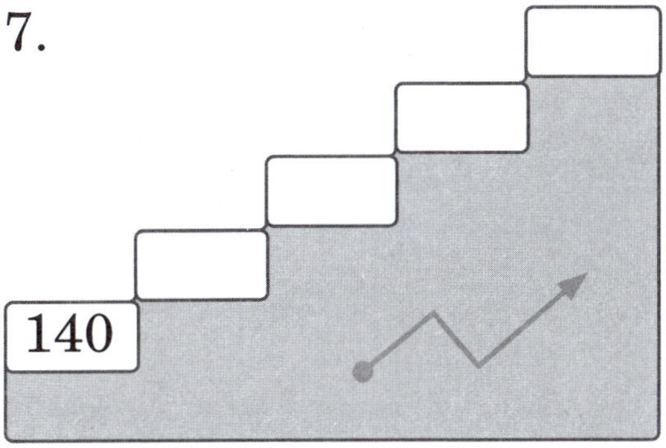

8.

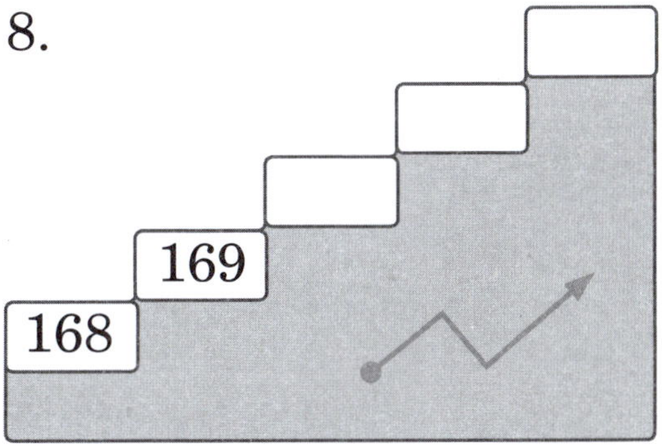

9.

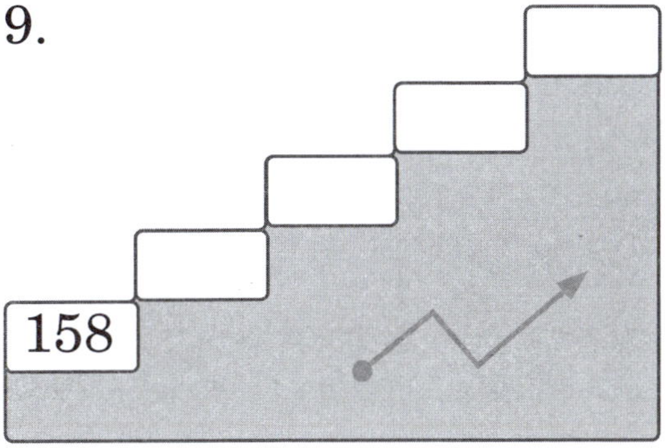

10.

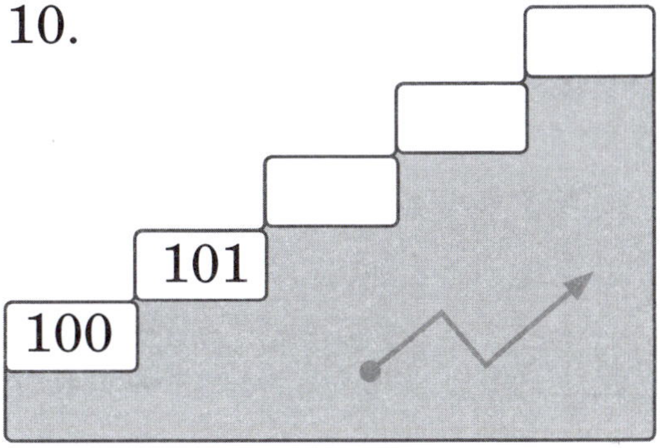

11.

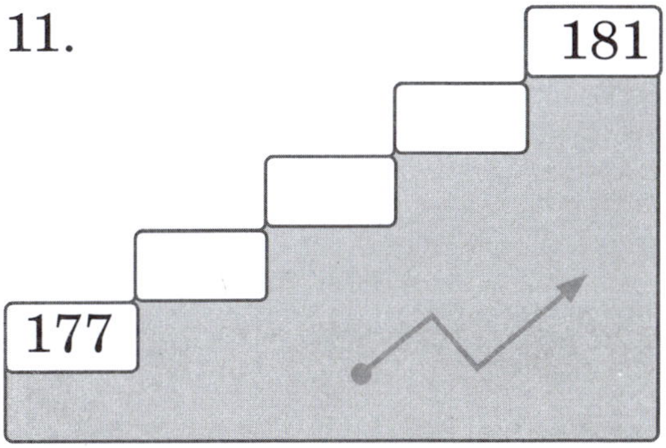

12.

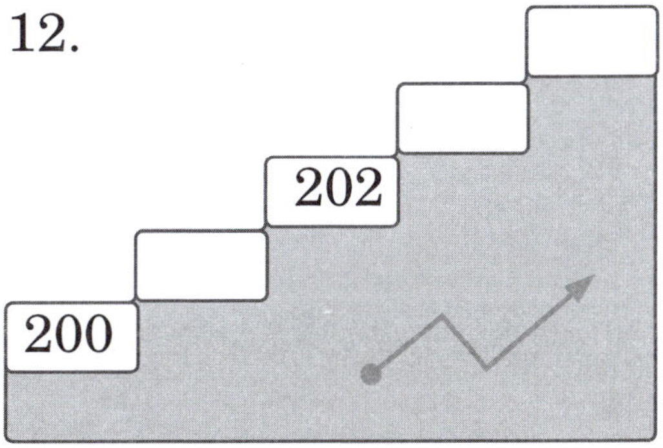

Date.................. Remarks.................... Signature....................

B. Practise more:

EXAMPLE:

1.

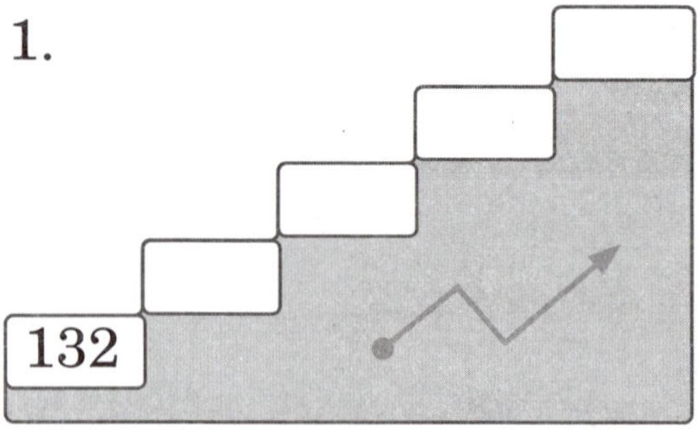

2.

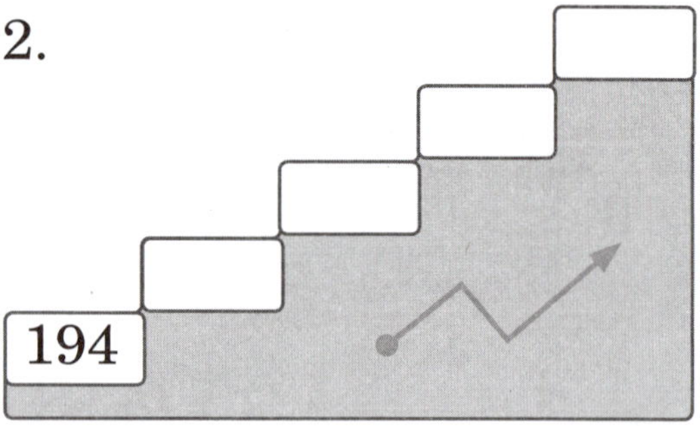

3.

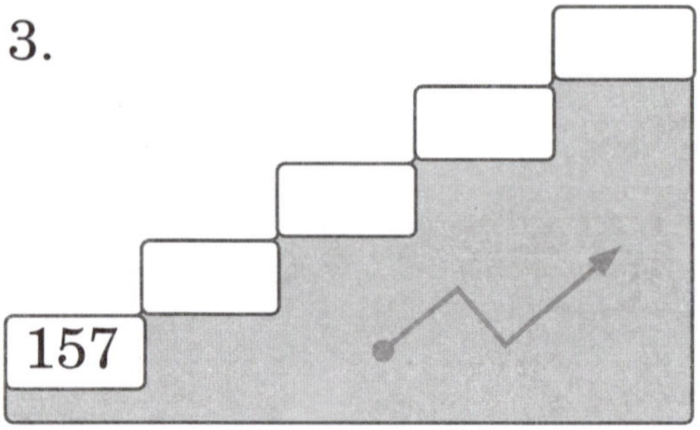

4.

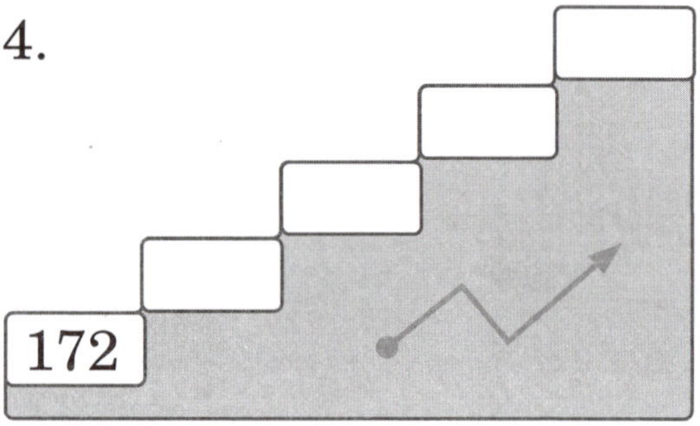

5.

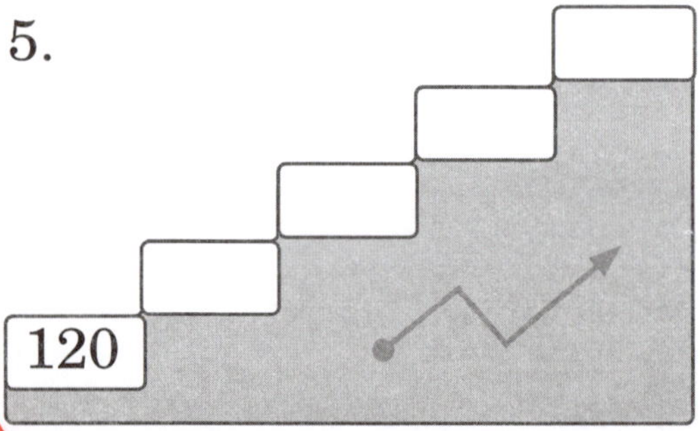

6.

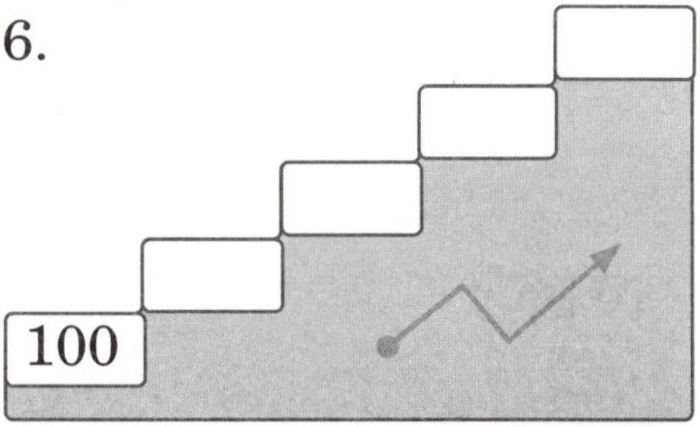

7.

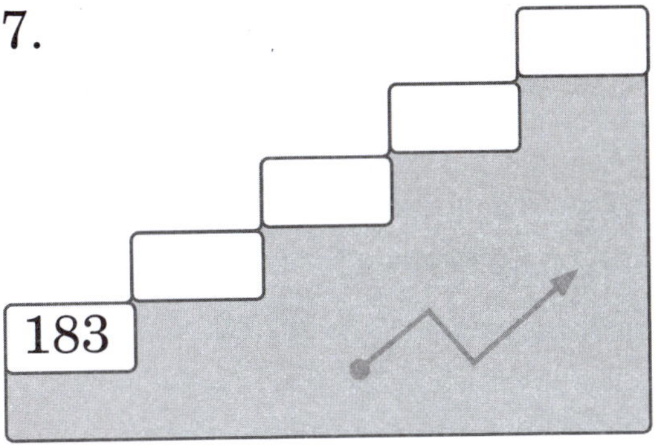

8.

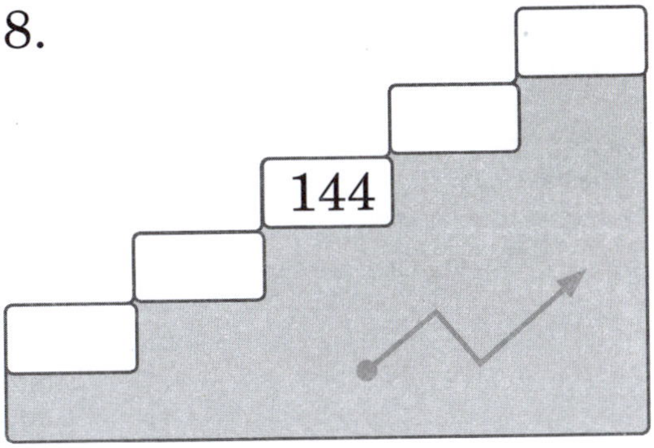

9.

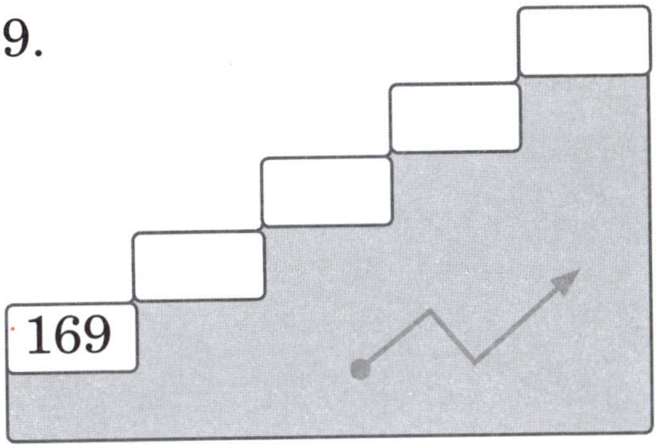

10.

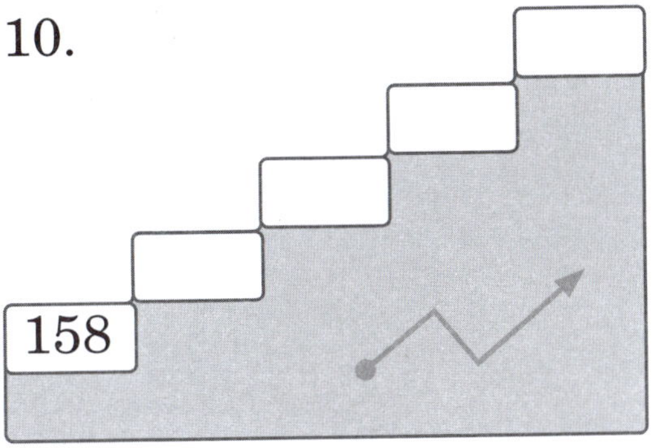

11.

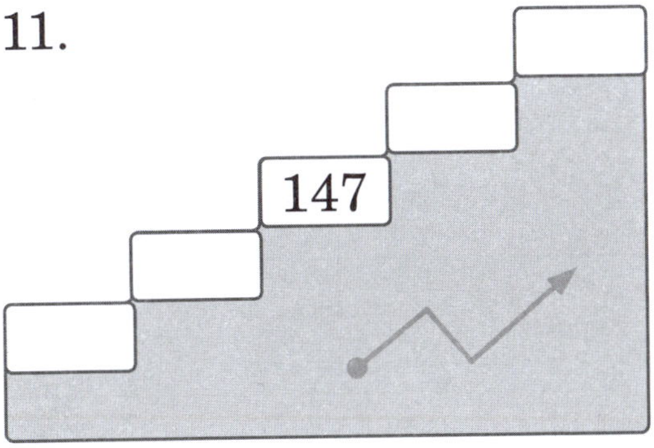

12.

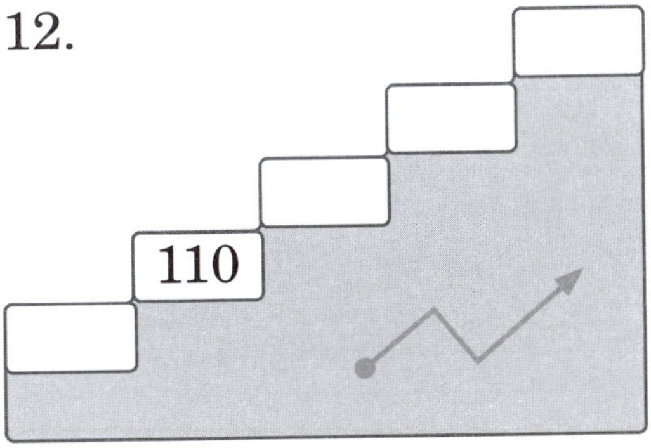

13.

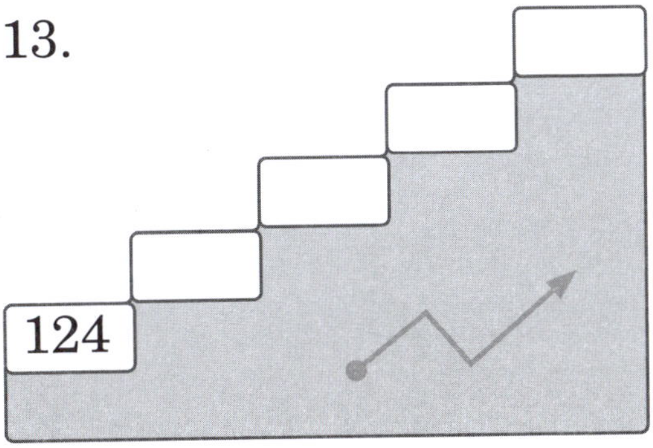

14.

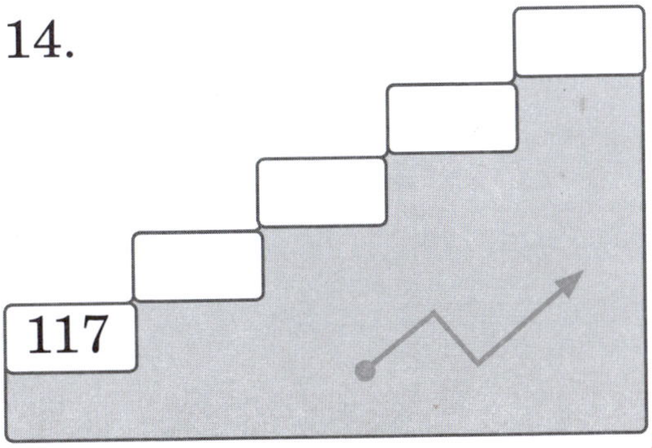

EXERCISE 8

DESCENDING ORDER

A. Write the numbers in descending order:

EXAMPLE:

1.

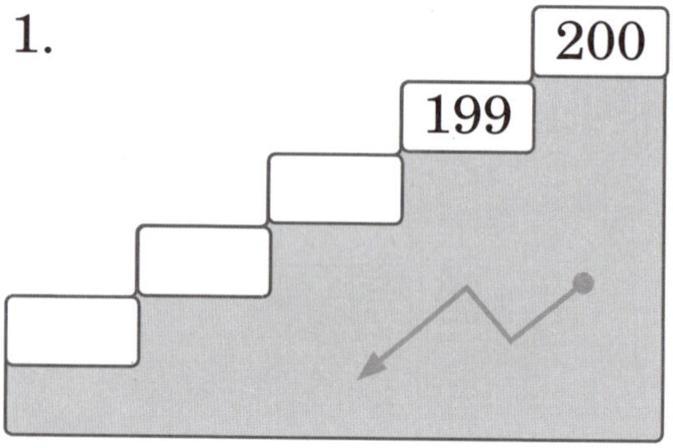

2.

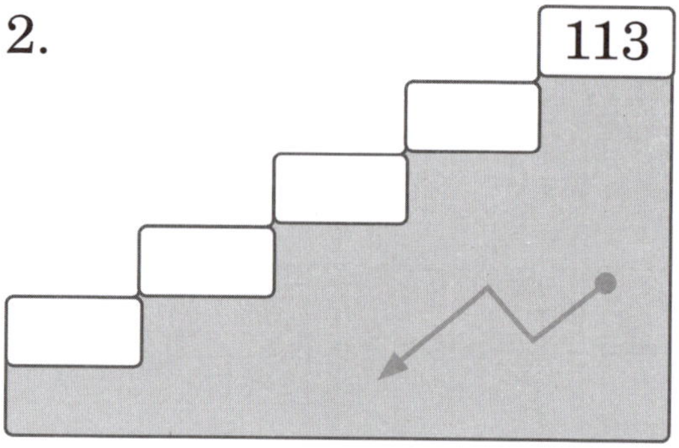

3.

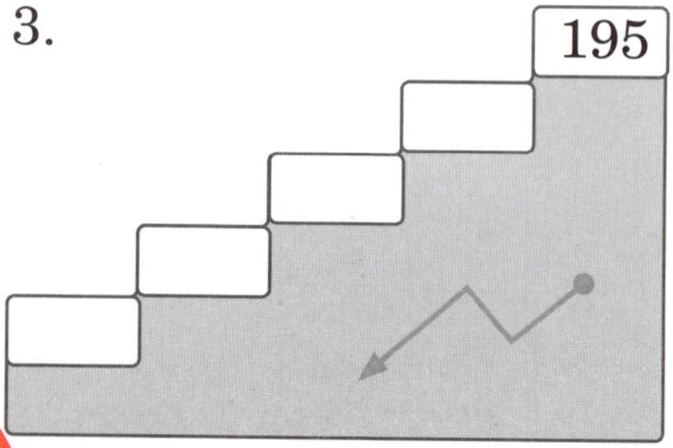

4.

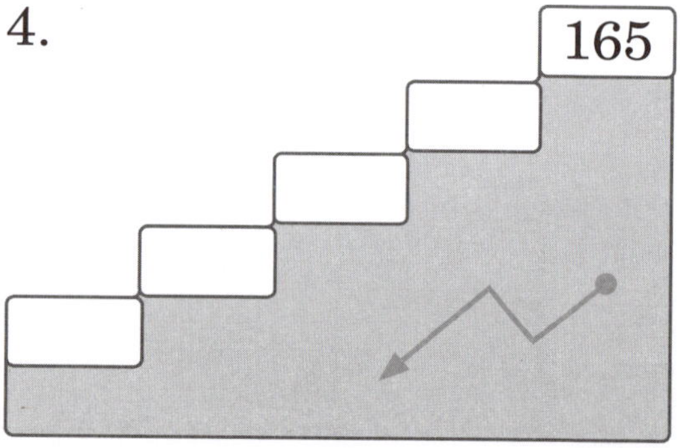

Date.................... Remarks...................... Signature......................

5.

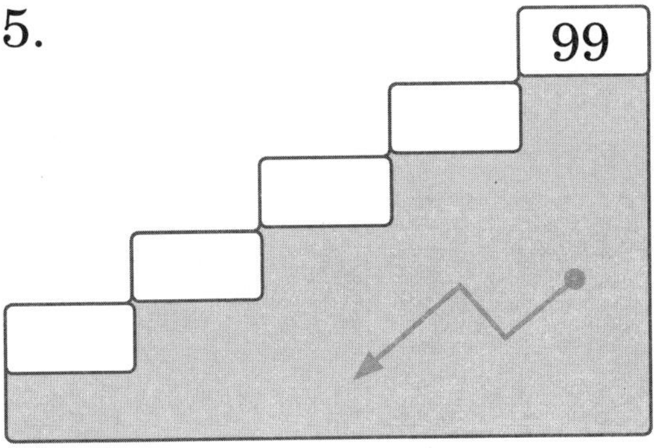

6.

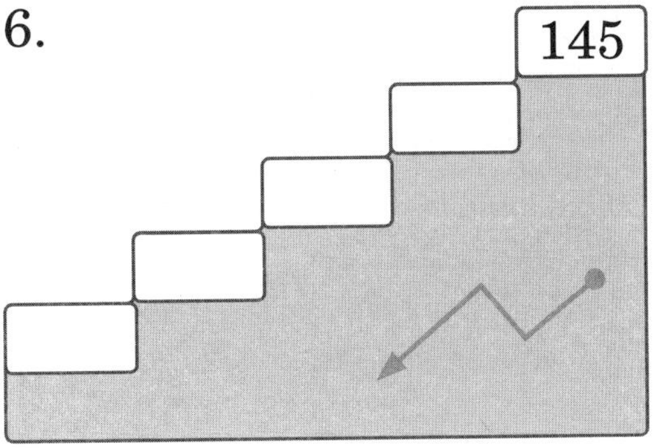

7.

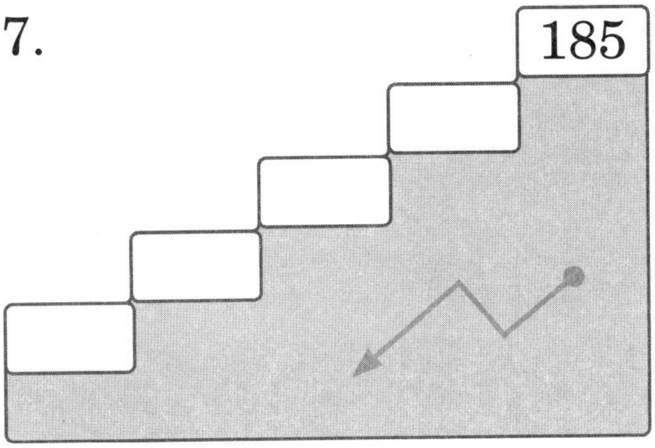

8.

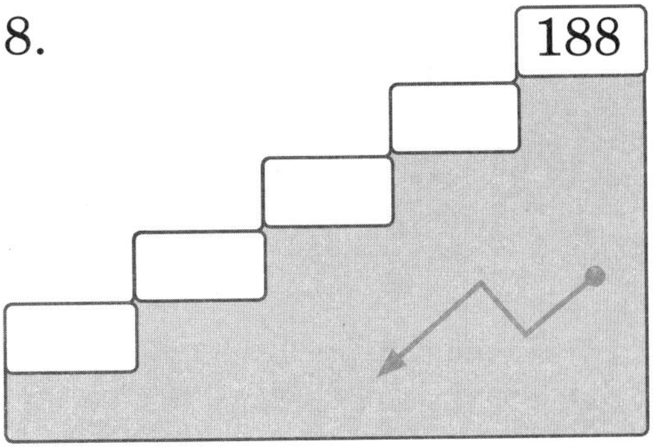

9.

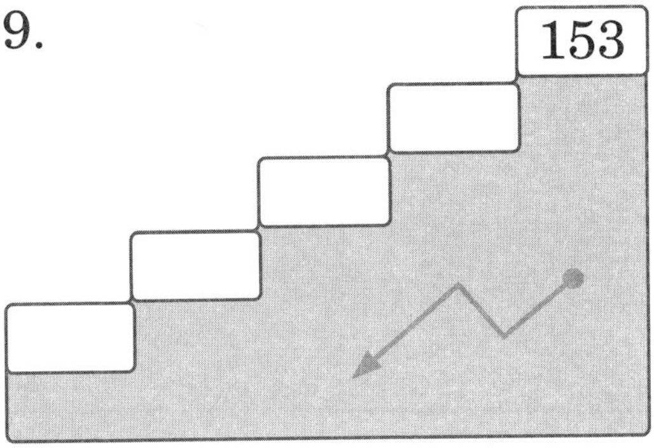

10.

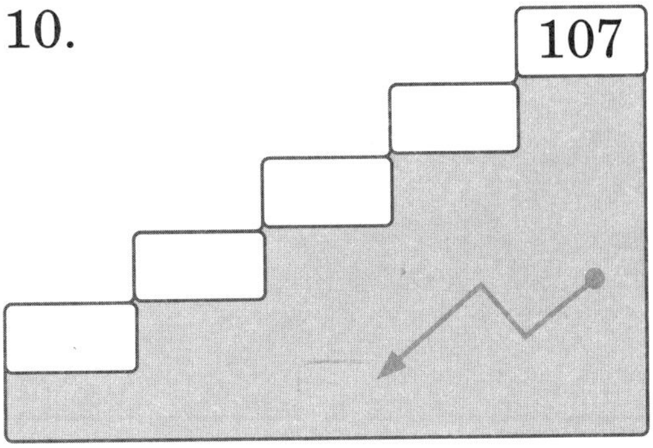

11.

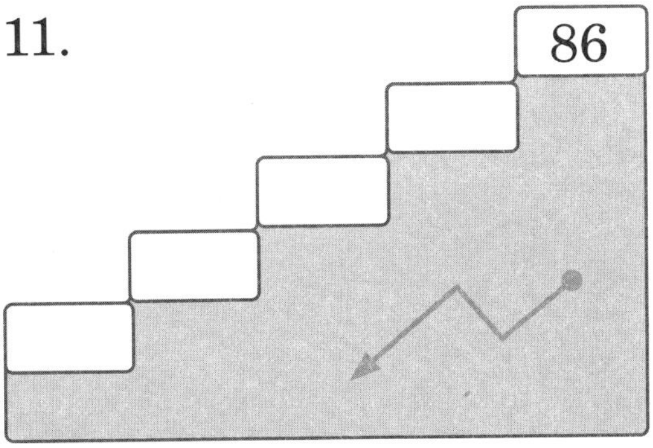

12.

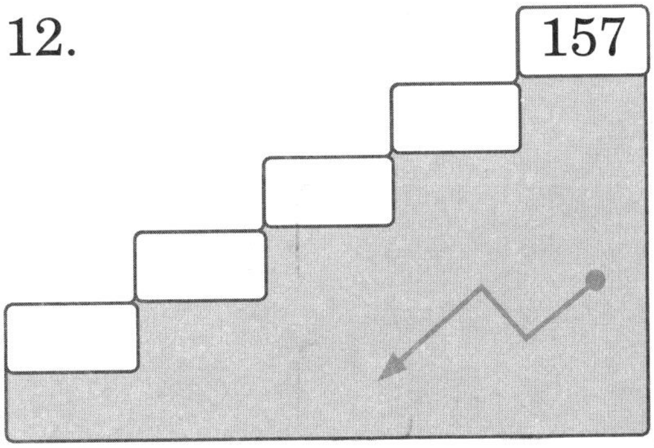

B. Practise more:

EXAMPLE:

146	149	150	148	147
150	149	148	147	146

1\.

128	127	125	129	126

2\.

162	161	165	163	164

3\.

198	196	200	199	197

4\.

188	184	187	185	186

5\.

173	177	174	176	175

6\.

119	120	123	122	121

Date.................... Remarks..................... Signature.....................

7.

156	159	160	158	157

8.

115	114	116	117	113

9.

169	167	168	170	166

10.

134	132	136	135	133

C. Write numbers in descending order:

EXAMPLE:

197	100	79	52	150
197	150	100	79	52

1.

70	30	50	60	40

2.

28	87	55	99	36

Date.................... Remarks..................... Signature.....................

3.	63	88	89	75	91
4.	149	129	123	158	188
5.	160	155	145	115	128
6.	169	200	199	109	139
7.	141	175	90	32	101
8.	54	39	65	28	96
9.	193	155	100	177	126
10.	118	198	109	189	138

Date.................. Remarks.................... Signature....................

EXERCISE 9

NUMBERS 201-300

Let's read and learn:

201	211	221	231	241	251	261	271	281	291
202	212	222	232	242	252	262	272	282	292
203	213	223	233	243	253	263	273	283	293
204	214	224	234	244	254	264	274	284	294
205	215	225	235	245	255	265	275	285	295
206	216	226	236	246	256	266	276	286	296
207	217	227	237	247	257	267	277	287	297
208	218	228	238	248	258	268	278	288	298
209	219	229	239	249	259	269	279	289	299
210	220	230	240	250	260	270	280	290	300

Date.................. Remarks...................... Signature.....................

EXERCISE 10

NUMBERS 301-400

Let's read and learn:

301	311	321	331	341	351	361	371	381	391
302	312	322	332	342	352	362	372	382	392
303	313	323	333	343	353	363	373	383	393
304	314	324	334	344	354	364	374	384	394
305	315	325	335	345	355	365	375	385	395
306	316	326	336	346	356	366	376	386	396
307	317	327	337	347	357	367	377	387	397
308	318	328	338	348	358	368	378	388	398
309	319	329	339	349	359	369	379	389	399
310	320	330	340	350	360	370	380	390	400

Date.................... Remarks..................... Signature.....................

EXERCISE 11

NUMBERS IN ORDER

A. Write the numbers in order:

EXAMPLE:

280 → 281 → 282 → 283

302 → 303 → 304 → 305

1. 370 → ___ → ___ → ___

2. ___ → 206 → ___ → ___

3. ___ → ___ → 211 → ___

4. 390 → ___ → ___ → ___

5. ___ → 370 → ___ → ___

6. ___ → ___ → ___ → 250

Date.................... Remarks...................... Signature......................

B. Write in order. Start from the smallest one:

EXAMPLE:

300 → 301 → 302 → 303 → 304

1.			199		
2.	210				
3.		309			
4.	377				
5.			269		
6.				250	
7.	379				
8.			305		
9.				299	

Date.................... Remarks...................... Signature......................

10.		360			
11.					217
12.		326			
13.				211	
14.		274			
15.				311	
16.		334			
17.			256		
18.	387				
19.					291
20.		280			

Date.................. Remarks.................... Signature....................

C. Write the following numbers in the increasing and decreasing order:

EXAMPLE:

207 208 206 209 205 204

Increasing order = 204, 205, 206, 207, 208, 209

Decreasing order = 209, 208, 207, 206, 205, 204

1. 318 316 314 317 315 313

   Increasing order ____________________

   Decreasing order ____________________

2. 251 254 256 255 253 252

   Increasing order ____________________

   Decreasing order ____________________

3. 326 328 327 329 330 325

   Increasing order ____________________

   Decreasing order ____________________

4. 300 297 296 299 301 298

   Increasing order ____________________

   Decreasing order ____________________

Date.................. Remarks.................... Signature....................

5. 192 194 195 196 193 191

Increasing order ____________________

Decreasing order ____________________

6. 275 278 276 277 274 279

Increasing order ____________________

Decreasing order ____________________

7. 181 179 180 183 182 178

Increasing order ____________________

Decreasing order ____________________

8. 374 377 375 376 378 373

Increasing order ____________________

Decreasing order ____________________

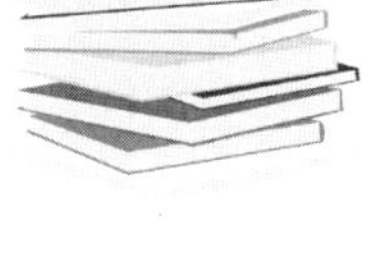

Date.................. Remarks.................... Signature....................

EXERCISE 12

SMALLEST NUMBER

A. Circle the smallest number and fill in the blanks:

EXAMPLE:

299 249 216 (201) 300 = 201

1.	225	277	363	200	340	=	
2.	300	361	282	374	101	=	
3.	50	19	11	201	98	=	
4.	32	42	22	12	52	=	
5.	376	255	244	100	99	=	
6.	16	15	10	80	98	=	
7.	77	54	55	85	70	=	
8.	399	299	199	209	129	=	
9.	70	17	98	58	78	=	
10.	84	20	62	78	40	=	

Date.................... Remarks..................... Signature.....................

B. Colour the smallest number in red:

EXAMPLE:

192 193 187 131 152

1.	142	131	182	123	143
2.	201	101	205	102	204
3.	327	336	380	342	320
4.	118	303	156	233	262
5.	238	371	228	316	299
6.	214	231	221	251	264
7.	177	396	231	100	216
8.	136	237	150	263	340

Date.................. Remarks.................... Signature....................

C. Underline the smallest number:

EXAMPLE:

28 85
19 <u>21</u> 36

32 <u>30</u>
65 71 41

1. 201 217
   210 211 199

2. 98 85
   74 65 62

3. 289 298
   117 189 107

4. 190 231
   234 315 200

5. 312 213
   370 330 234

6. 234 345
   211 198 250

7. 67 98
   56 78 49

8. 191 98
   129 313 122

Date.................. Remarks.................... Signature....................

EXERCISE 13

BIGGEST NUMBER

A. Circle the biggest number and fill in the blanks:

EXAMPLE:

	197	209	(400)	99	386	= 400
1.	202	399	112	302	80	= ☐
2.	97	65	55	91	81	= ☐
3.	366	266	66	86	346	= ☐
4.	255	99	378	189	202	= ☐
5.	115	300	73	95	212	= ☐
6.	199	99	399	299	98	= ☐
7.	303	103	186	288	299	= ☐
8.	95	201	105	200	159	= ☐
9.	96	286	308	88	198	= ☐
10.	255	373	271	117	200	= ☐

Date.................... Remarks..................... Signature.....................

B. Write the biggest and smallest number:

EXAMPLE:

						BIGGEST	SMALLEST
123	114	156	214	312	=	312	114

							BIGGEST	SMALLEST
1.	99	38	46	101	25	=		
2.	310	212	108	346	100	=		
3.	48	34	62	26	96	=		
4.	303	150	340	290	80	=		
5.	136	240	90	176	300	=		
6.	163	281	303	93	76	=		
7.	143	287	201	199	302	=		
8.	368	244	159	188	323	=		
9.	321	369	123	36	262	=		
10.	288	388	188	186	248	=		

Date.................... Remarks..................... Signature.....................

EXERCISE 14

ADDITION

A. Add and write the missing answers:

EXAMPLE:

16 + 5 = 21

23 + 21 = 44

1. 6 + 11 = ◯
2. 2 + 1 = ◯
3. 21 + 31 = ◯
4. 19 + 4 = ◯
5. 10 + 30 = ◯
6. 18 + 5 = ◯
7. 33 + 20 = ◯
8. 12 + 8 = ◯
9. 27 + 3 = ◯
10. 25 + 13 = ◯

Date.................... Remarks..................... Signature.....................

B. Add the following numbers:

EXAMPLE:

39	30 + 9	
50	40 + 10	

1. 26 + 12 = ☐
2. 12 + 48 = ☐
3. 0 + 25 = ☐
4. 7 + 16 = ☐
5. 13 + 17 = ☐
6. 30 + 10 = ☐
7. 22 + 13 = ☐
8. 5 + 19 = ☐
9. 20 + 14 = ☐
10. 17 + 3 = ☐

Date.................. Remarks..................... Signature.....................

C. Add the numbers in such a way so that the answer is 12:

6 + ☐ = 12

4 + ☐ = 12

8 + ☐ = 12

7 + ☐ = 12

9 + ☐ = 12

3 + ☐ = 12

D. Write the missing answers:

1. 5 + 5 = ◯
2. 5 + 2 = ◯
3. 6 + 4 = ◯
4. 9 + 7 = ◯
5. 3 + 8 = ◯
6. 1 + 5 = ◯

Date.................... Remarks..................... Signature.....................

EXERCISE 15

SUBTRACTION

Subtract and write the difference:

EXAMPLE:

48 − 22 = 26

35 − 13 = 22

1. 43 − 11 = ______
2. 98 − 41 = ______
3. 59 − 23 = ______
4. 46 − 32 = ______
5. 55 − 20 = ______
6. 67 − 42 = ______
7. 88 − 31 = ______
8. 38 − 16 = ______
9. 25 − 15 = ______
10. 86 − 23 = ______

Date.................. Remarks.................... Signature....................

B. Subtract and write the answer:

EXAMPLE:

23 – 12 = 11

38 – 23 = 15

1. 63 – 30 =

2. 26 – 15 =

3. 96 – 85 =

4. 76 – 53 =

5. 68 – 32 =

6. 86 – 34 =

7. 73 – 42 =

8. 49 – 27 =

9. 83 – 41 =

10. 94 – 51 =

Date.................... Remarks..................... Signature.....................

EXERCISE 16

FUN WITH ADDITION

Do the following addition:

EXAMPLE:

13 = [6] + 7 | 20 = 9 + [11] | [18] = 8 + 10

1. 25 = 10 + ☐

2. 30 = ☐ + 20

3. ☐ = 17 + 8

4. 12 = ☐ + 4

5. 20 = ☐ + 9

6. ☐ = 18 + 10

7. 12 = 3 + ☐

8. 18 = ☐ + 4

9. ☐ = 13 + 20

10. 15 = ☐ + ☐

Date.................... Remarks...................... Signature......................

B. Practise more:

EXAMPLE:

9 + 5 = 14	18 + 5 = 23	33 = 13 + 20

1.	☐	+	8	=	22
2.	23	+	12	=	☐
3.	14	+	☐	=	21
4.	☐	+	19	=	29
5.	☐	+	27	=	39
6.	7	+	☐	=	15
7.	☐	+	4	=	59
8.	23	+	☐	=	37
9.	32	+	☐	=	48
10.	13	+	☐	=	36

Date.................... Remarks...................... Signature......................

EXERCISE 17

FUN WITH SUBTRACTION

Find the missing number:

EXAMPLE:

19 – 4 = (15) | (18) – 8 = 10 | 34 – (21) = 13

1.	15	–	☐	=	6
2.	☐	–	11	=	9
3.	18	–	6	=	☐
4.	22	–	☐	=	13
5.	17	–	10	=	☐
6.	19	–	15	=	☐
7.	11	–	☐	=	11
8.	16	–	☐	=	14
9.	8	–	☐	=	2
10.	14	–	6	=	☐

Date.................. Remarks.................... Signature....................

B. Study the example and find the missing number:

EXAMPLE:

17 – (4) = 13   (37) – 8 = 29   26 – 13 = (13)

1. 18 – 9 = ☐
2. ☐ – 6 = 8
3. 11 – ☐ = 7
4. 23 – 7 = ☐
5. ☐ – 15 = 5
6. 12 – ☐ = 12
7. ☐ – 17 = 3
8. 27 – 14 = ☐
9. 36 – ☐ = 7
10. 24 – ☐ = 11

Date.................... Remarks..................... Signature.....................

EXERCISE 18

NUMBERS 401- 500

Let's read and learn:

401	411	421	431	441	451	461	471	481	491
402	412	422	432	442	452	462	472	482	492
403	413	423	433	443	453	463	473	483	493
404	414	424	434	444	454	464	474	484	494
405	415	425	435	445	455	465	475	485	495
406	416	426	436	446	456	466	476	486	496
407	417	427	437	447	457	467	477	487	497
408	418	428	438	448	458	468	478	488	498
409	419	429	439	449	459	469	479	489	499
410	420	430	440	450	460	470	480	490	500

Date.................... Remarks..................... Signature.....................

EXERCISE 19

FUN WITH MISSING NUMBERS

A. Fill in the blanks with missing numbers:

EXAMPLE:

	263		265		→	262	263	264	265	266	
308					→	308	309	310	311	312	

1.				230		
2.	434				438	
3.			377			
4.	322					
5.		299				
6.	166	167				
7.	385					
8.	416					
9.			487			
10.			183			

Date.................. Remarks.................... Signature....................

A. Complete the number chain as shown in the example:

EXAMPLE:

303 → 304 → 305 → 306 → 307

432 → 433 → 434 → 435 → 436

1.	243				
2.			383	384	
3.		299		301	
4.	361				365
5.				350	
6.	456				
7.			411		
8.		488			491
9.	266				
10.				219	

Date................... Remarks..................... Signature.....................

EXERCISE 20

NUMBER PATTERNS

A. Circle the patterns and write them in the blanks:

EXAMPLE:

(26)	38	33	(27)	20	=	26	27
42	28	(35)	58	(34)	=	34	35

1.	36	99	35	73	66	=		
2.	61	77	88	23	89	=		
3.	12	51	32	96	52	=		
4.	72	63	73	27	58	=		
5.	144	189	101	190	156	=		
6.	66	50	63	49	52	=		
7.	97	88	76	90	87	=		
8.	47	44	48	40	42	=		
9.	93	39	45	89	38	=		
10.	60	51	55	59	57	=		

Date.................... Remarks..................... Signature....................

B. Write more patterns in the blanks:

EXAMPLE:

296	342	297	310	298	=	296	297	298
430	401	399	410	400	=	399	400	401

1.	161	272	388	270	271	=			
2.	176	182	180	170	181	=			
3.	320	327	311	326	325	=			
4.	500	498	360	219	499	=			
5.	188	199	189	170	190	=			
6.	288	277	275	280	276	=			
7.	444	446	445	380	440	=			
8.	299	298	305	310	297	=			
9.	119	129	125	118	120	=			
10.	361	388	377	362	363	=			

Date.................... Remarks..................... Signature.....................

C. Complete the pattern:

EXAMPLE:

2	4	6	8	10	12	14	16
88	77	66	55	44	33	22	11

1.	3	6	9		15	18		
2.	10	12	14				22	
3.	11		33		55			
4.	18	17	16			13		11
5.	10	20			50			80
6.	4	8	12		20		28	32
7.			71	61	51			21
8.	15	25		45		65		
9.	39	37	35			29	27	
10.	5	7		11	13			19

Date.................. Remarks..................... Signature.....................

EXERCISE 21
ADDITION FACTS

A. Fill in the blanks by writing the correct answers:

EXAMPLE:

9	9	→	18
12	6	→	18

10	12	→	22
8	14	→	22

1.

10	10	→	
14	6	→	

2.

13	4	→	
11	6	→	

3.

8	3	→	
7	4	→	

4.

11	2	→	
8	5	→	

5.

12	3	→	
9	6	→	

6.

15	4	→	
10	9	→	

7.

6	3	→	
2	7	→	

8.

16	14	→	
30	0	→	

9.

14	4	→	
10	8	→	

10.

7	9	→	
1	15	→	

Date.................... Remarks...................... Signature......................

EXAMPLE:

15	20	5
12	20	8

8	16	8
15	16	1

1.

8	19	11
	19	9

2.

3	11	
6	11	5

3.

14		12
11		3

4.

4	12	
6	12	6

5.

5	10	5
	10	10

6.

13	18	
9	18	9

7.

7	14	7
8	14	

8.

13	17	4
	17	7

9.

		10
6	13	7

10.

11		5
	16	8

Date.................. Remarks.................... Signature....................

C. Study the pattern and complete the following:

EXAMPLE:

40	↓	20
	20	

25	↑	30
	55	

1.

14	↑	13

2.

13	↓	25

3.

50	↓	31

4.

10	↑	23

5.

18	↓	12

6.

22	↑	12

7.

14	↓	27

8.

27	↑	27

9.

16	↑	13

10.

36	↓	23

11.

17	↓	17

12.

18	↑	28

13.

18	↓	5

14.

38	↓	18

15.

20	↑	20

Date.................. Remarks.................... Signature....................

EXERCISE 22

SUBTRACTION FACTS

A. Study the pattern and do the following sums:

EXAMPLE:

28 - 5 = 23   4 = 14 - 18

1. 38 - ___ = 30
2. ___ - 7 = 13
3. 27 - 11 = ___
4. ___ - 14 = 6
5. 31 - 8 = ___
6. 27 - ___ = 16
7. 19 - 5 = ___

8 7 = 25 - ___

9. 10 = ___ - 23
10. 5 = ___ - 15
11. ___ = 17 - 34
12. ___ = 12 - 26
13. 4 = ___ - 37
14. ___ = 11 - 14

Date.................. Remarks..................... Signature.....................

B. Do more sums:

EXAMPLE:

Balloon	Balloon	Box
38	15	23
28	12	16
30	20	10

No.	Balloon	Balloon	Box
1.	35		16
2.	27		19
3.	24	11	
4.		13	10
5.	24		13
6.	28	8	
7.	36	18	
8.	34		11
9.		22	9

Date.................... Remarks..................... Signature......................

10.	18	9	
11.	38		16
12.		15	7

C. Study the pattern of addition and subtraction and practise more:

EXAMPLE:

30 + 10 = 40 | 28 - 17 = 11

1.	18 +		48	6.	42 -		14
2.		+ 18	19	7.	27 -	0	
3.	16 +		36	8.	37 -		25
4.	15 +		25	9.	29 -		20
5.	13 +		32	10.		- 22	16

Date.................... Remarks..................... Signature.....................

EXERCISE 23

MONEY

A. Count the coins and tick the correct option:

₵ stands for currency

EXAMPLE:

5 + 2 + 10

a. ₵14 b. ₵13 c. ₵17 d. ₵15

1. 5 + 1 + 2

a. ₵10 b. ₵3 c. ₵8 d. ₵5

2. 10 + 5 + 10

a. ₵30 b. ₵25 c. ₵27 d.₵26

3. 10 + 10 + 10

a. ₵40 b. ₵50 c. ₵30 d. ₵65

4. 10 + 2 + 25

a. ₵40 b. ₵50 c. ₵60 d. ₵37

Date.................... Remarks..................... Signature.....................

5. 5 + 5 + 10

a. ₵40 b. ₵20 c. ₵60 d. ₵35

6. 10 + 25 + 25

a. ₵50 b. ₵30 c. ₵60 d. ₵35

7. 25 + 5 + 10

a. ₵40 b. ₵30 c. ₵50 d. ₵35

8. 2 + 5 + 10

a. ₵40 b. ₵30 c. ₵57 d. ₵35

9. 10 + 5 + 1

a. ₵18 b. ₵16 c. ₵17 d. ₵15

10. 50 + 25 + 25

a. ₵100 b. ₵80 c. ₵120 d. ₵90

Date.................. Remarks.................... Signature....................

B. Count the money pictured to determine how much the item costs:

1. Peter buys apple, strawberry, pineapple and mixed fruit jams from the market. How much money does he have to pay if the jams cost ₵6, ₵8, ₵6 and ₵7 each?

----

2. Audrey bought fruits worth ₵6, ₵10 and ₵15. How much money did she spend in total?

----

3. Edgar bought 3 packets of different types of dog food. If each packets cost ₵8, how much money did he pay in total?

Date.................. Remarks.................... Signature....................

Look at the price of each item. Write the total amount to be paid. If you give ₵100 to the shopkeeper each time, calculate the change that you will receive.

₵5

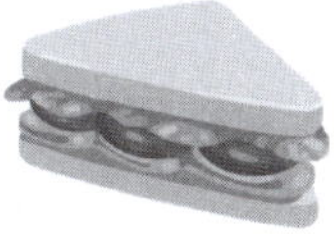

₵30

₵15

₵25

Purchase Food	**Amount to be paid**	**How much change?**

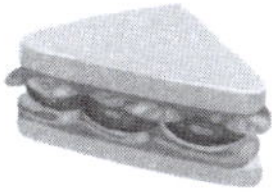 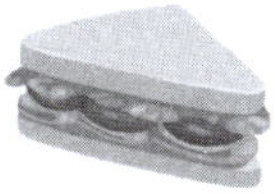		

Date.................. Remarks.................... Signature....................

EXERCISE 24
SHAPES

A. Let's learn shapes:

Oval

Triangle

Circle

Square

Rectangle

Star

Straight Line

Slanting Line

Curved Line

Date.................. Remarks.................... Signature....................

B. Match the correct shapes:

Oval ●	●
Square ●	●
Circle ●	●
Star ●	●
Rectangle ●	●
Triangle ●	●

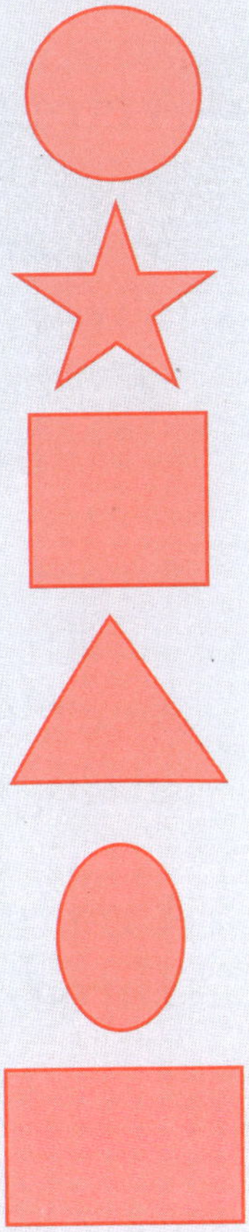

C. Draw any 4 shapes and colour them:

Date.................... Remarks..................... Signature.....................

D. Learn more about shapes by choosing the correct option from the brackets:

1. A circle looks like a __________. (bat, ball, basket)
2. A square has _______________ equal sides. (three, five, four)
3. A triangle has __________ sides. (four, two, three)
4. A rectangle has _________ corners. (four, six, five)
5. A circle has ______________ line. (straight, slanting, curved)
6. A rectangle has____________ equal sides. (three, two, four)

E. Name the following shapes:

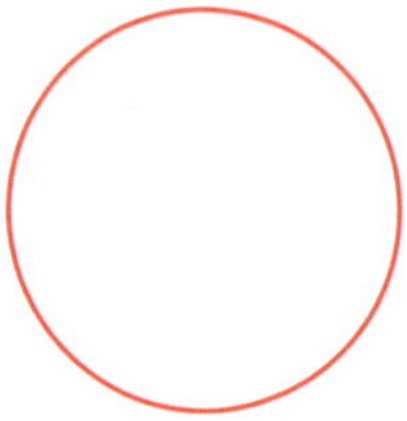

....

....

....

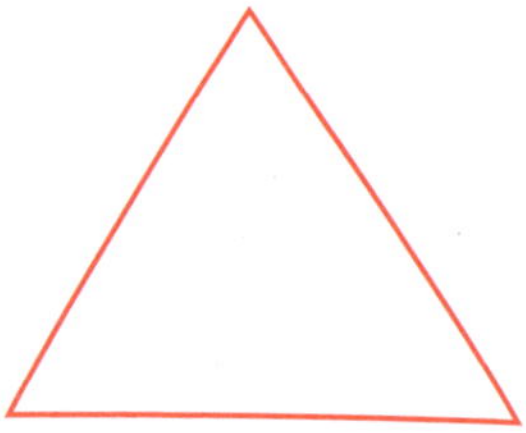

....

....

....

Date.................. Remarks.................... Signature....................

EXERCISE 25

NUMBER NAMES 1-20

A. Let's read and learn:

NUMBER	NAME	NUMBER	NAME
1	One	11	Eleven
2	Two	12	Twelve
3	Three	13	Thirteen
4	Four	14	Fourteen
5	Five	15	Fifteen
6	Six	16	Sixteen
7	Seven	17	Seventeen
8	Eight	18	Eighteen
9	Nine	19	Nineteen
10	Ten	20	Twenty

Date.................... Remarks...................... Signature......................

B. Fill in the blanks:

1	o n e	11	e _ e _ e n
2	t _ o	12	t w _ l v _
3	t h _ _ e	13	t h _ r t e e n
4	f _ _ r	14	f o _ _ t e e n
5	f _ _ e	15	f i _ t e e n
6	s _ x	16	s i _ t e e n
7	s _ v _ n	17	s e _ e _ t e e n
8	e _ g _ t	18	e i _ h t e e n
9	n _ n e	19	n _ n _ t e _ n
10	t _ n	20	t _ _ n t y

C. Match the following numbers to their names:

18	nineteen
15	sixteen
13	eighteen
19	fifteen
16	thirteen

Date.................... Remarks.................... Signature....................

D. Write words and numbers in the blanks:

EXAMPLE:

8 = eight 14 = fourteen

8	=		three	=	
7	=		six	=	
10	=		one	=	
4	=		nine	=	
6	=		five	=	
3	=		seven	=	
1	=		ten	=	
2	=		eight	=	
9	=		two	=	
5	=		four	=	

E. Write more:

15	=		twelve	=	
12	=		eleven	=	
17	=		nineteen	=	
13	=		eighteen	=	

Date.................. Remarks.................... Signature.....................

D. Write the numbers:

1. Twenty-two	
2. Thirty-seven	
3. Twenty	
4. Forty-two	
5. Nineteen	
6. Thirty-eight	
7. Twenty-one	
8. Forty-six	
9. Twenty-three	
10. Thirty-nine	

Date.................. Remarks.................... Signature....................

EXERCISE 26
CODES

A. Let's learn coding:

w	e	h	n	i	x	r	t	v	s	f	o
1	2	3	4	5	6	7	8	9	10	11	12

EXAMPLE:

six = 10 5 6

1. two = ☐ ☐ ☐
2. nine = ☐ ☐ ☐ ☐
3. three = ☐ ☐ ☐ ☐ ☐
4. five = ☐ ☐ ☐ ☐
5. ten = ☐ ☐ ☐
6. one = ☐ ☐ ☐
7. seven = ☐ ☐ ☐ ☐ ☐

Date.................. Remarks.................... Signature....................

B. Do more coding:

r	u	t	v	w	f	e	o	n	i	h	y
1	2	3	4	5	6	7	8	9	10	11	12

EXAMPLE:

8 9 7 = o n e

1. 6 8 2 1
2. 3 5 8
3. 6 10 4 7
4. 9 10 9 7
5. 3 11 1 7 7
6. 3 11 10 13 7 7 9
7. 6 10 6 3 12
8. 3 5 7 9 3 12
9. 3 11 10 1 3 12
10. 9 10 9 7 3 7 7 9

Date.................. Remarks..................... Signature.....................

C. Practise more coding:

l	s	u	r	n	f	e	t	h	o	w	i	v	x
1	2	3	4	5	6	7	8	9	10	11	12	13	14

EXAMPLE:

eleven = 7 1 7 13 7 5   four = 6 10 3 4

1. twelve
2. fifteen
3. seventeen
4. fourteen
5. sixteen
6. 5 12 5 7 8 7 7 5
7. 8 9 12 4 8 7 7 5
8. 2 12 14

Date.................... Remarks.................... Signature....................

D. Complete the following:

o	t	f	w	x	i	n	v	h	u	y	r	g	e	s
1	2	3	4	5	6	7	8	9	10	11	12	13	14	15

EXAMPLE:

7 6 7 14 = n i n e

1. 15 14 8 14 7

☐ ☐ ☐ ☐ ☐

2. 1 7 14

☐ ☐ ☐

3. 14 6 13 9 2

☐ ☐ ☐ ☐ ☐

4. 2 4 14 7 2 11

☐ ☐ ☐ ☐ ☐ ☐

5. 3 6 8 14

☐ ☐ ☐ ☐

Date.................. Remarks..................... Signature.....................

6. 2 4 7

7. 14 6 13 9 2 14 14 7

8. 2 4 14 7 2 11 2 4 1

9. 3 1 10 12

10. 2 9 6 12 2 14 14 7

11. 2 9 12 14 14

12. 3 6 3 2 14 14 7

Date................... Remarks..................... Signature.....................

13. 3 1 12 2 11

14. 2 9 6 12 2 11 1 7 14

15. 2 4 14 7 2 11 15 14 8 14 7

16. 7 6 7 14 2 14 14 7

17. 2 9 6 12 2 11 3 6 8 14

18. 15 14 8 14 7 2 14 14 7

Date.................. Remarks.................... Signature....................

EXERCISE 27

NUMBER NAMES 21-50

A. Let's read and learn:

NUMBER	NAME	NUMBER	NAME	NUMBER	NAME
21	twenty-one	31	thirty-one	41	forty-one
22	twenty-two	32	thirty-two	42	forty-two
23	twenty-three	33	thirty-three	43	forty-three
24	twenty-four	34	thirty-four	44	forty-four
25	twenty-five	35	thirty-five	45	forty-five
26	twenty-six	36	thirty-six	46	forty-six
27	twenty-seven	37	thirty-seven	47	forty-seven
28	twenty-eight	38	thirty-eight	48	forty-eight
29	twenty-nine	39	thirty-nine	49	forty-nine
30	thirty	40	forty	50	fifty

Date.................. Remarks.................... Signature....................

B. Complete these:

EXAMPLE:

27 = twenty-seven 35 = thirty-five 40 = forty

1. 25 t___enty-five
2. 33 t___irty-three
3. 42 fo___ty-two
4. 26 twen___y-six
5. 30 thi___ty
6. 24 t___enty-f___ur
7. 48 fo___ty-eight
8. 21 twe___ty-o_e
9. 14 fo___rteen
10. 19 ni___eteen
11. 28 t___enty-ei__ht
12. 38 th___rty-eight
13. 49 f___rty-nine
14. 32 thi___ty-two
15. 43 for___y-three
16. 46 fo___ty-six
17. 29 ___wenty-nine
18. 41 fort___-one
19. 39 ___hirty-nine
20. 37 t___enty-se__en

Date.................. Remarks.................... Signature....................

C. Write in words and numbers:

EXAMPLE:

28 = twenty-eight   34 = thirty-four

1. 32 =
2. 26 =
3. 39 =
4. 21 =
5. 44 =
6. 50 =
7. 23 =
8. 22 =
9. 47 =
10. 35 =
11. thirty-three =
12. forty-eight =
13. thirty-six =
14. twenty-four =
15. forty-two =
16. thirty-eight =
17. twenty-five =
18. forty-one =
19. thirty-seven =
20. fifty =

Date.................... Remarks..................... Signature.....................

EXERCISE 28

MULTIPLICATION TABLE

A. Let's learn multiplication tables:

How many times 2?

1. 1 time 2 is $1 \times 2 = 2$
2. 2 times 2 is $2 \times 2 = 4$
3. 3 times 2 is $3 \times 2 = 6$
4. 4 times 2 is $4 \times 2 = 8$
5. 5 times 2 is $5 \times 2 = 10$
6. 6 times 2 is $6 \times 2 = 12$
7. 7 times 2 is $7 \times 2 = 14$

Date.................. Remarks.................... Signature....................

8. 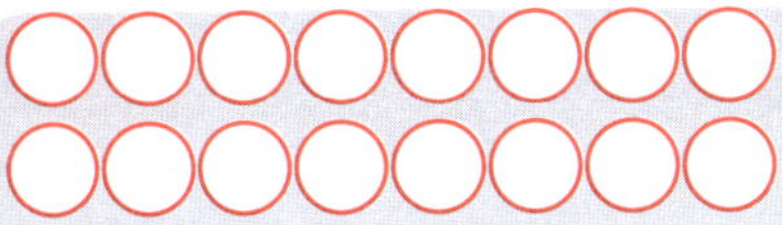 8 times 2 is 8 x 2 = 16

9. 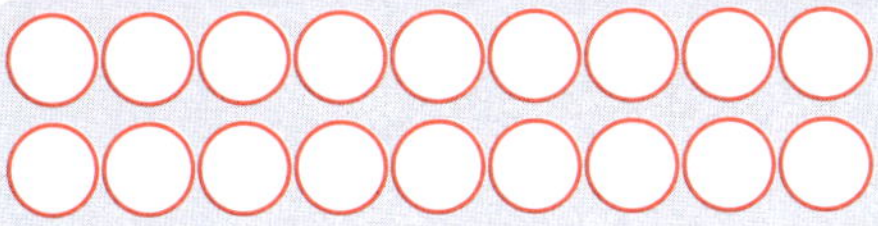 9 times 2 is 9 x 2 = 18

10. 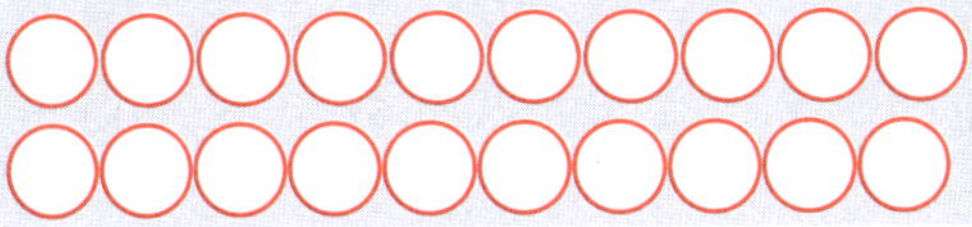 10 times 2 is 10 x 2 = 20

B. Learn the tables of 3, 4 and 5:

3	x	1	=	3
3	x	2	=	6
3	x	3	=	9
3	x	4	=	12
3	x	5	=	15
3	x	6	=	18
3	x	7	=	21
3	x	8	=	24
3	x	9	=	27
3	x	10	=	30

4	x	1	=	4
4	x	2	=	8
4	x	3	=	12
4	x	4	=	16
4	x	5	=	20
4	x	6	=	24
4	x	7	=	28
4	x	8	=	32
4	x	9	=	36
4	x	10	=	40

5	x	1	=	5
5	x	2	=	10
5	x	3	=	15
5	x	4	=	20
5	x	5	=	25
5	x	6	=	30
5	x	7	=	35
5	x	8	=	40
5	x	9	=	45
5	x	10	=	50

Date.................... Remarks..................... Signature.....................

C. Match the answers:

1.	5	x	3	18
2.	3	x	4	15
3.	2	x	8	30
4.	3	x	6	16
5.	4	x	5	12
6.	3	x	7	20
7.	3	x	10	21
8.	5	x	8	8
9.	4	x	2	45
10.	5	x	9	40

D. Jump 2 steps at a time to learn more:

4 times 2 is = 8

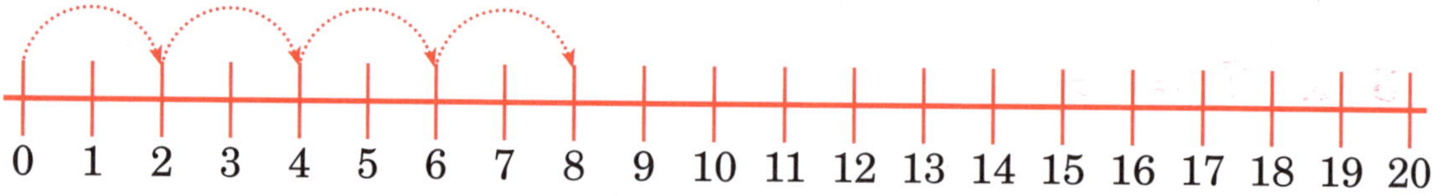

1. 3 times 2 is ______

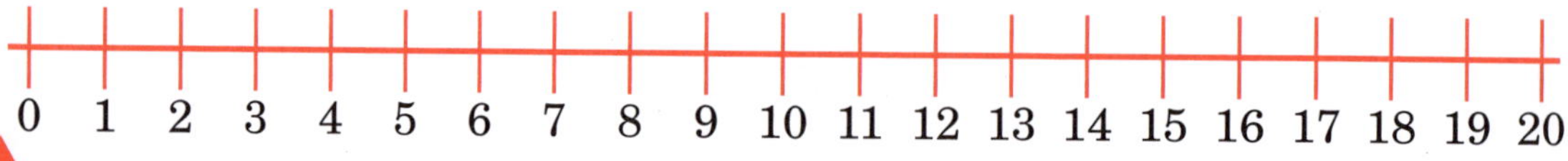

Date.................. Remarks.................... Signature....................

2. 5 times 2 is ☐

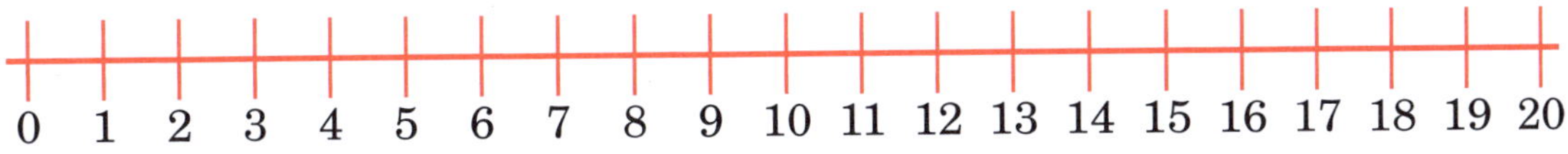

3. 8 times 2 is ☐

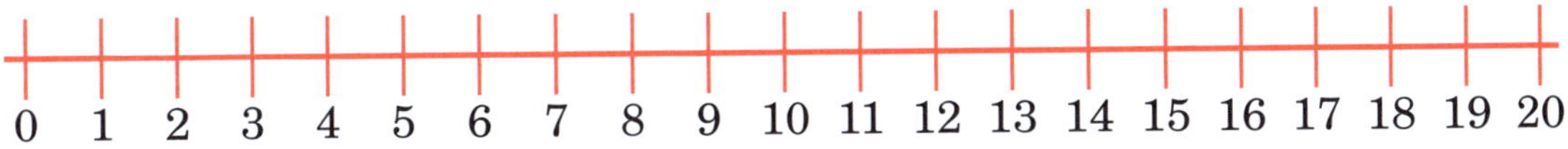

4. 6 times 2 is ☐

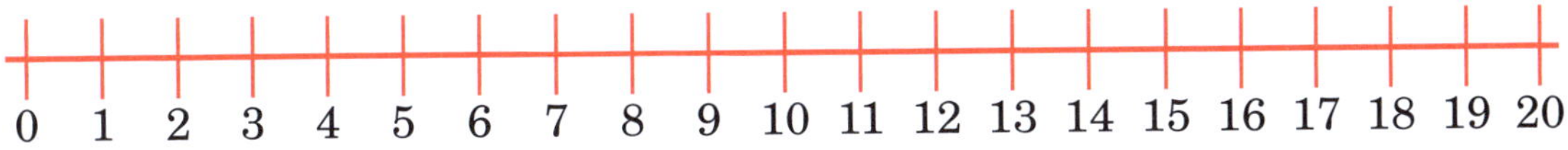

5. 9 times 2 is ☐

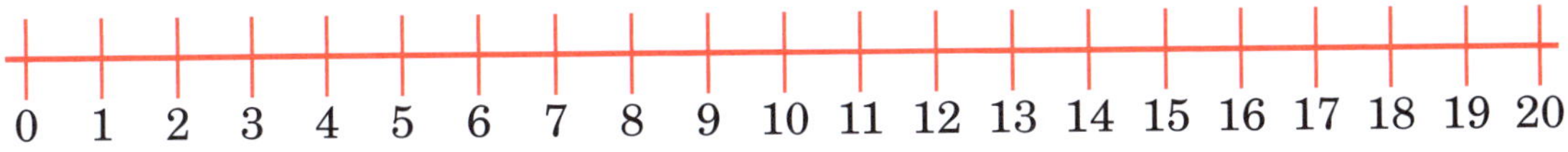

E. Practise more:

EXAMPLE:

2 → 4 → 6 → 8 → 10 → 12

1. ☐ → 8 → 12 → ☐ → 20 → ☐

2. 15 → ___ → 21 → ___ → 27 → ___

3. 25 → ___ → 35 → 40 → ___ → ___

4. ___ → 16 → 20 → ___ → ___ → ___

5. 9 → ___ → 15 → ___ → 21 → ___

6. 10 → ___ → ___ → 25 → ___ → ___

7. ___ → 15 → 18 → ___ → 24 → ___

8. 4 → ___ → 12 → ___ → ___ → 24

9. 10 → 12 → ___ → ___ → ___ → 20

10. ___ → 10 → 15 → ___ → ___ → ___

Date.................. Remarks.................... Signature....................

C. Match the answers:

EXAMPLE:

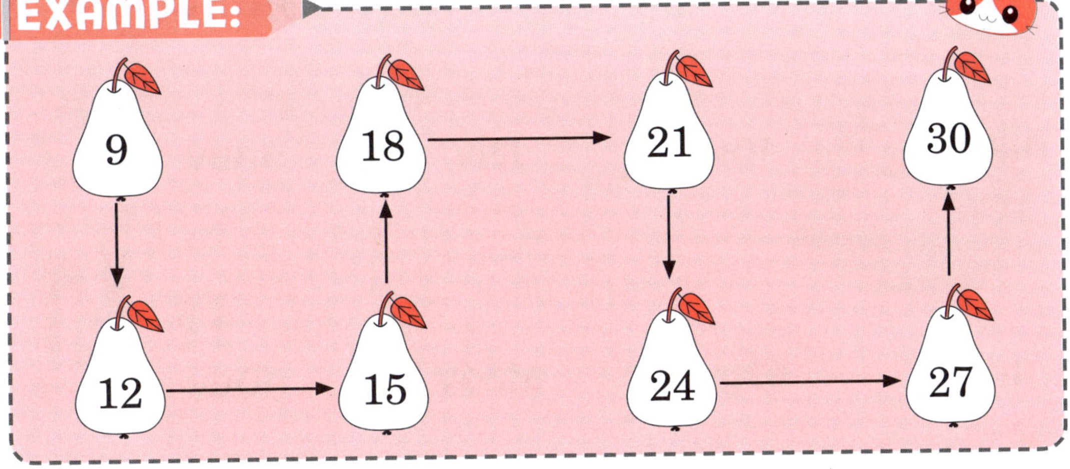

1.

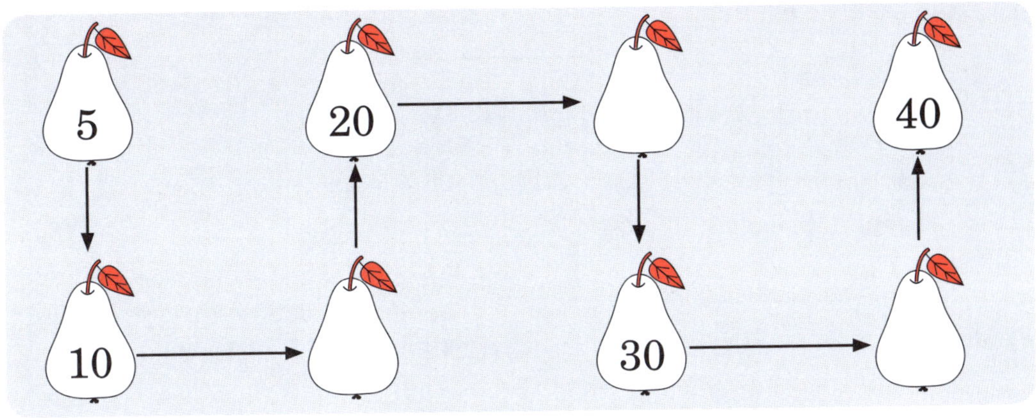

2.

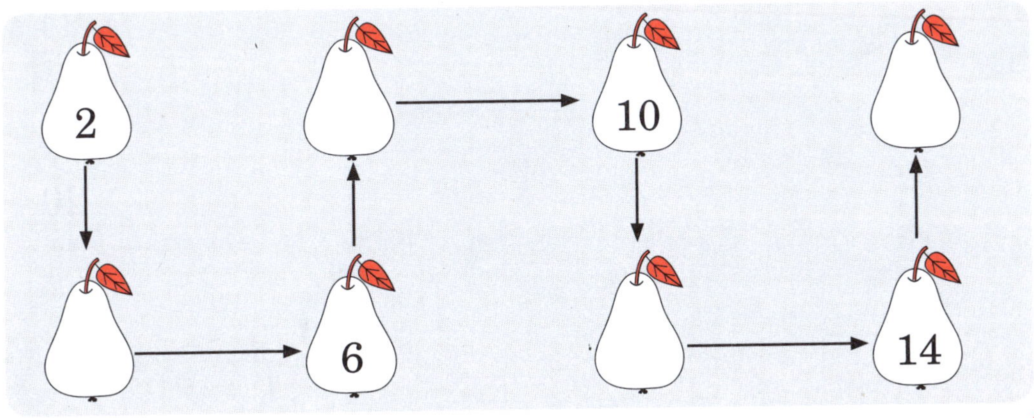

Date.................. Remarks.................... Signature....................

3.

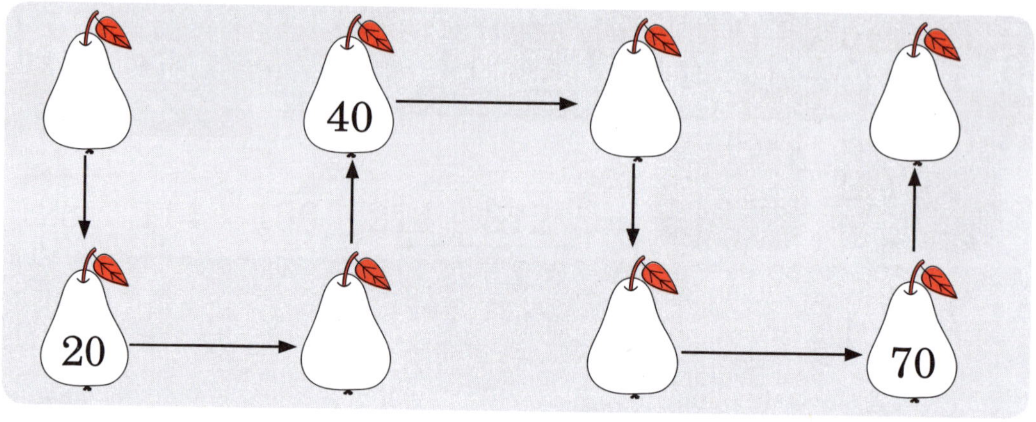

4.

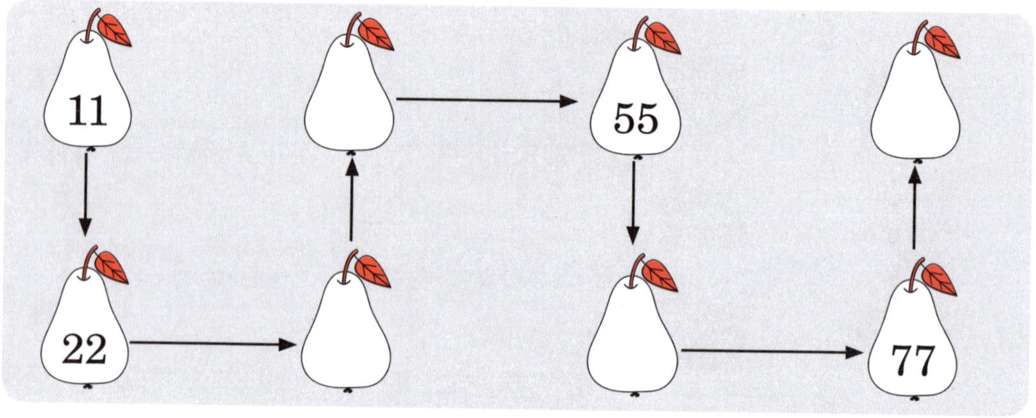

5.

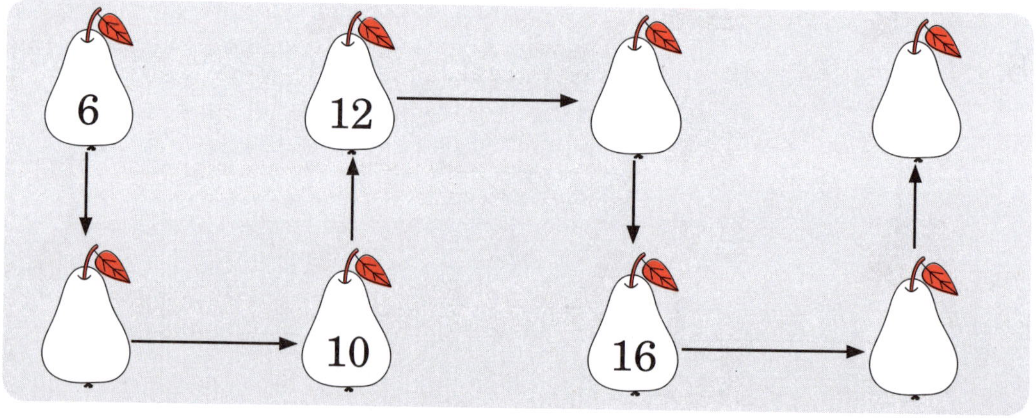

Date.................. Remarks.................... Signature.....................

6.

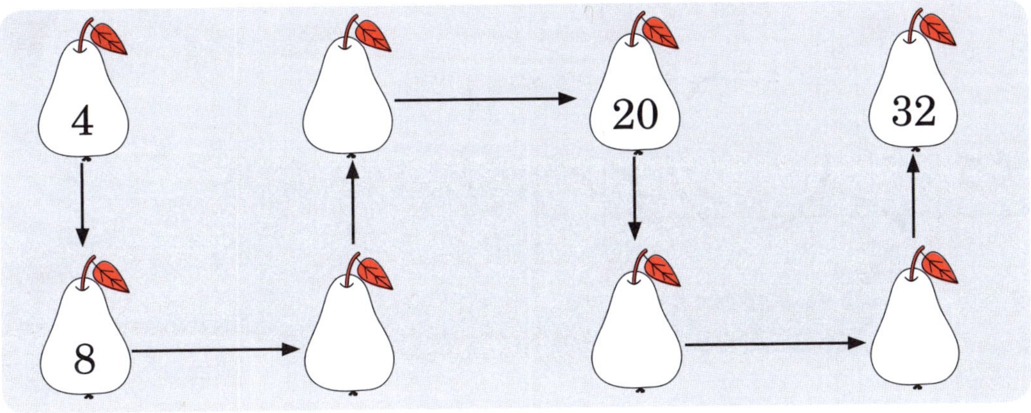

7.

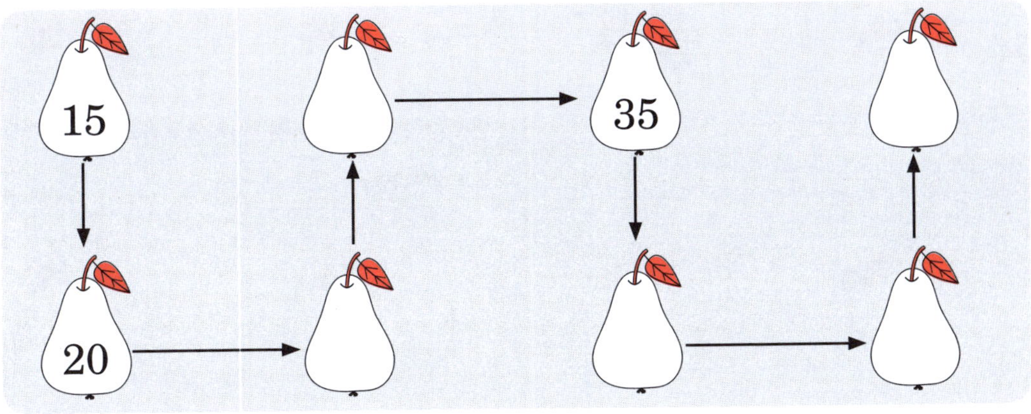

8.

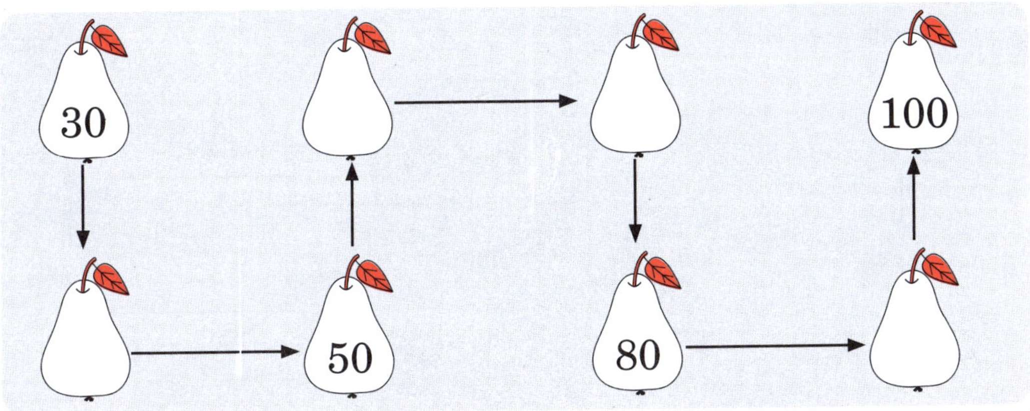

Date.................. Remarks.................... Signature....................

9.

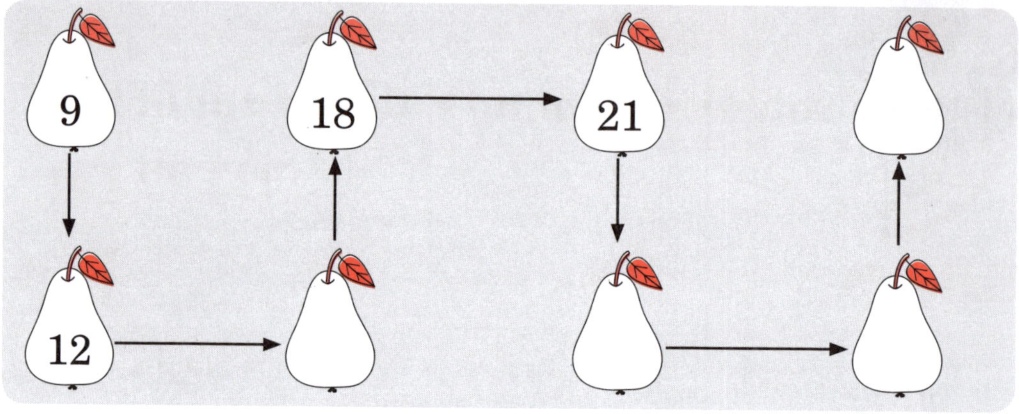

10.

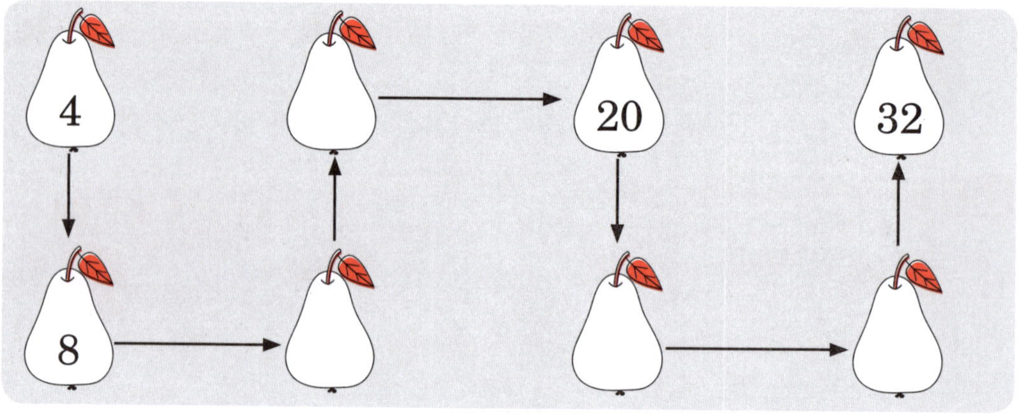

11.

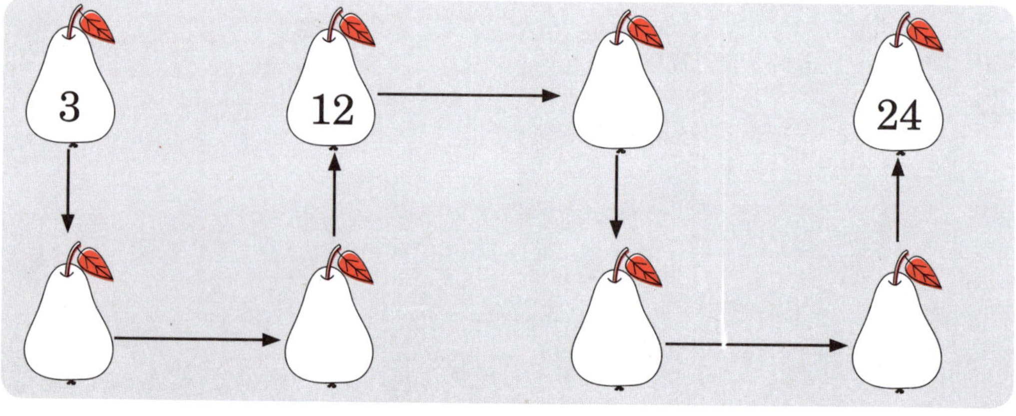

Date.................... Remarks...................... Signature......................

EXERCISE 29

FRACTIONS

A. Let's learn fractions:

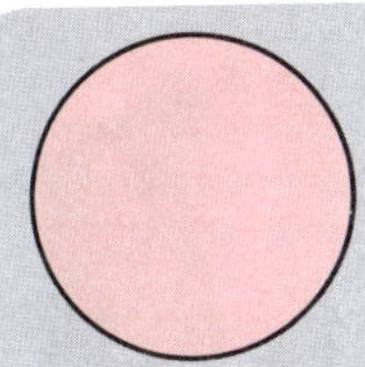

1

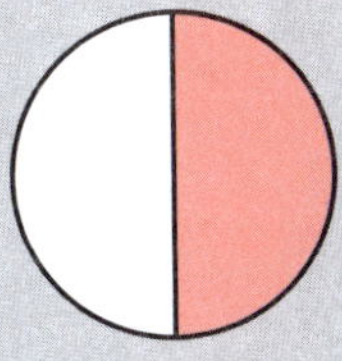

$\frac{1}{2}$

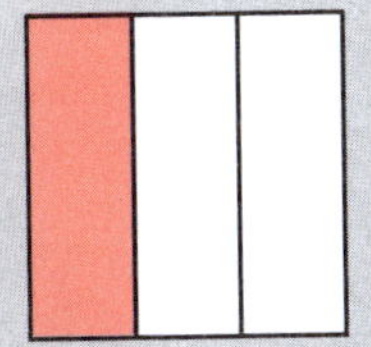

$\frac{1}{3}$

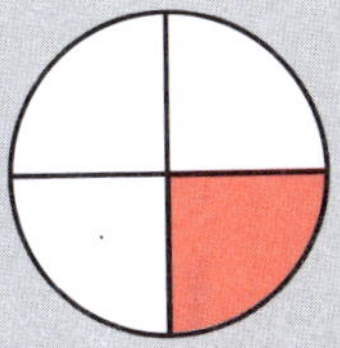

$\frac{1}{4}$

B. Colour the parts of the fractions:

1. 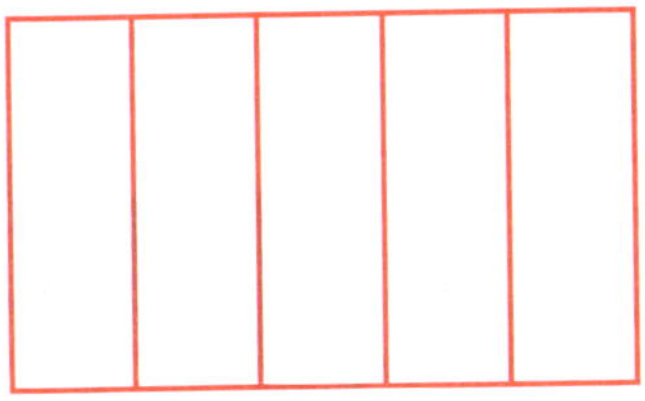

$\frac{1}{5}$

2. 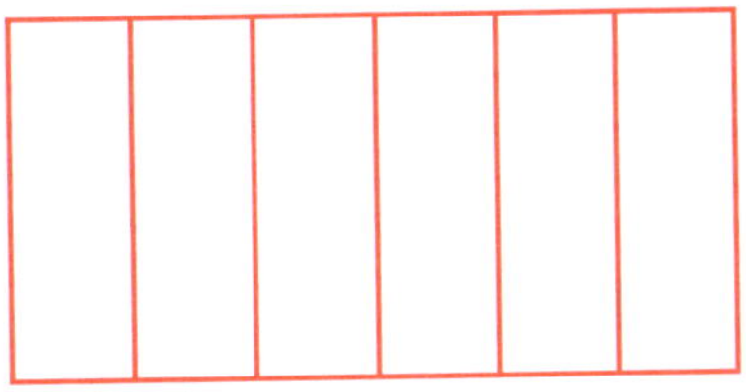

$\frac{1}{6}$

3. 

$\frac{1}{3}$

4. 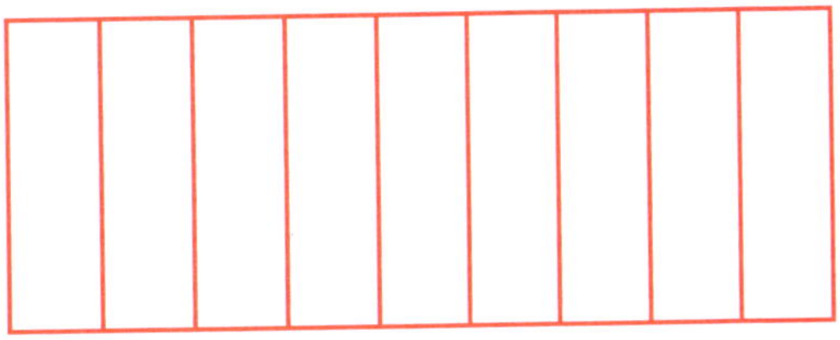

$\frac{1}{9}$

Date..................

Remarks.....................

Signature.....................

5.

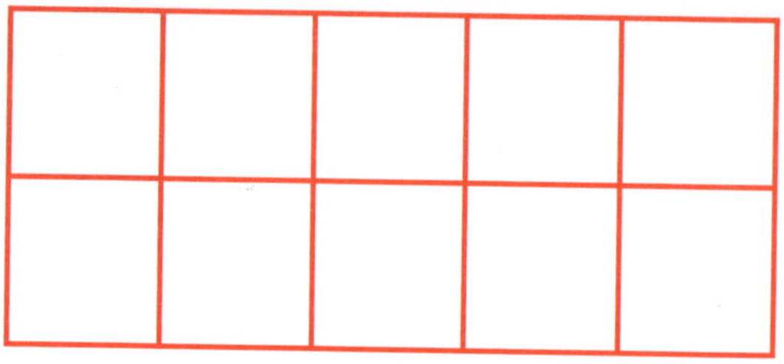

$\frac{1}{10}$

6.

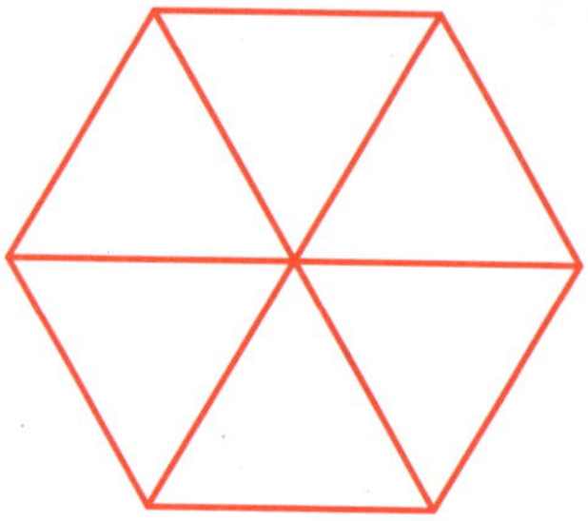

$\frac{1}{7}$

7.

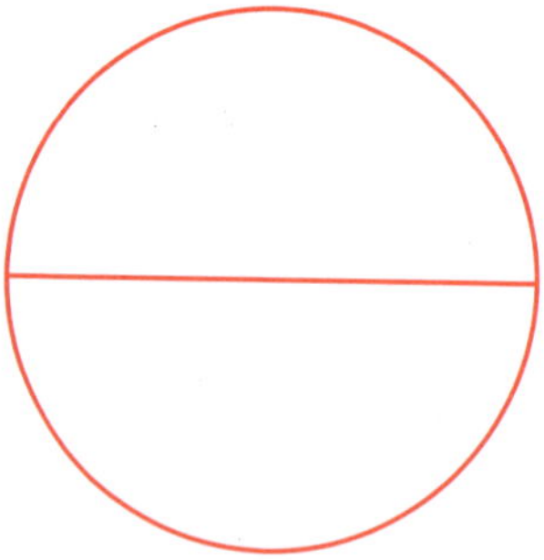

$\frac{1}{2}$

8.

$\frac{1}{4}$

9.

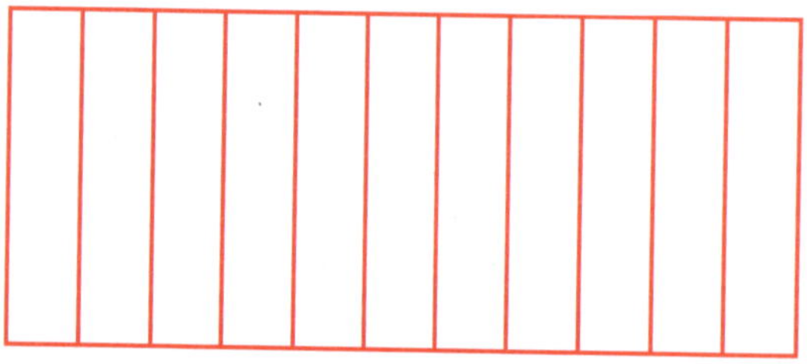

$\frac{1}{11}$

10.

$\frac{1}{8}$

Date.................. Remarks..................... Signature.....................

C. Divide these shapes into halves. Colour one half of each shape:

D. Write the fractions of the shaded part:

EXAMPLE:

1 $\quad \frac{1}{2}$ $\quad \frac{1}{4}$

1. 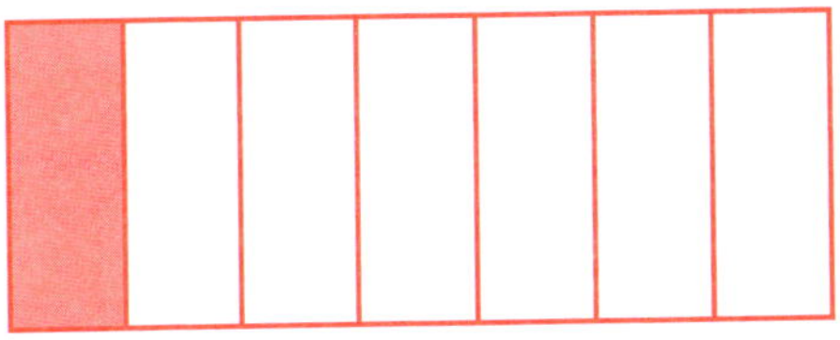

$\frac{\square}{\square}$

2. 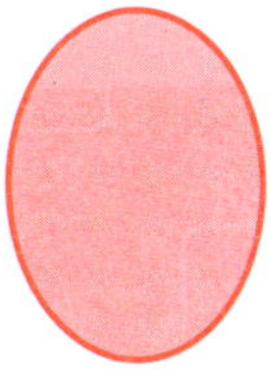

Date.................... Remarks..................... Signature.....................

3.

—

4.

—

5.

—

6.

—

7.

—

8.

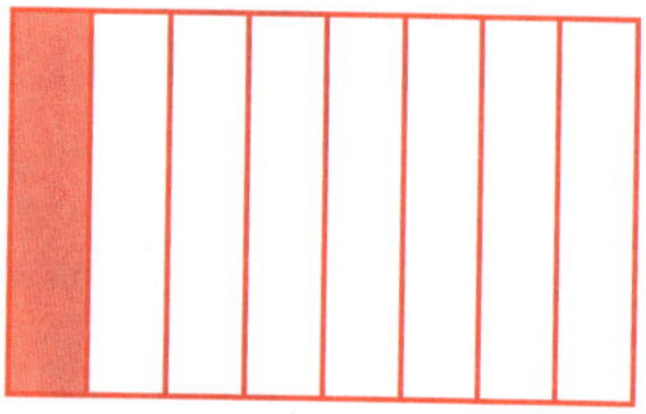

—

D. Write more fractions:

EXAMPLE:

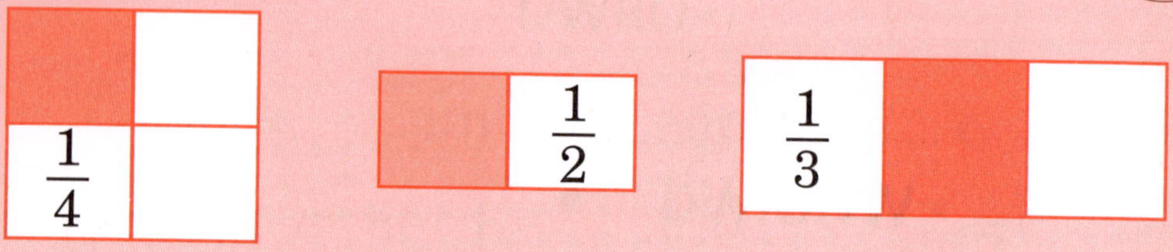

1.

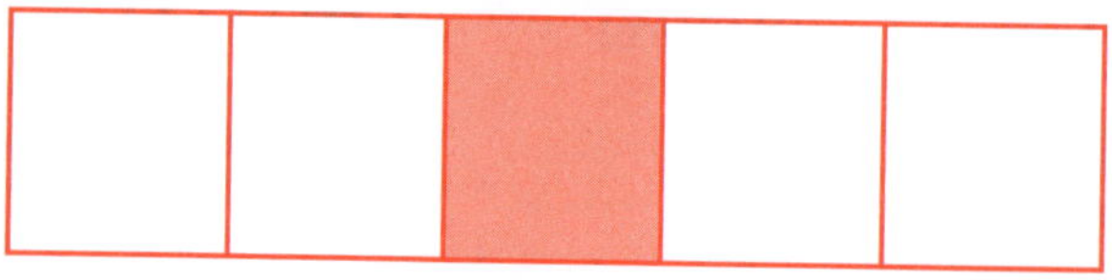

—

2.

—

Date...................   Remarks.....................   Signature.....................

3. 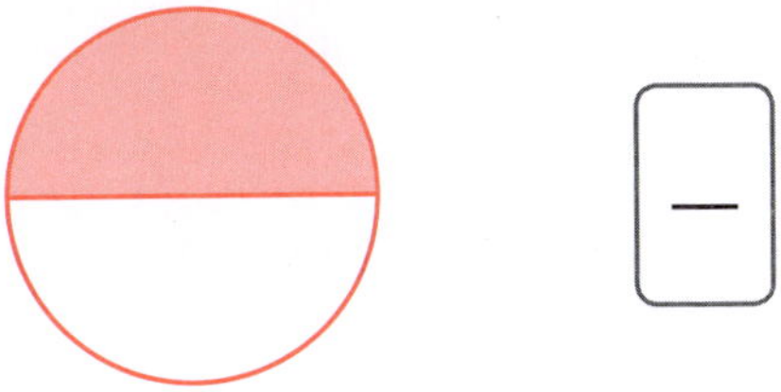

4. 

5 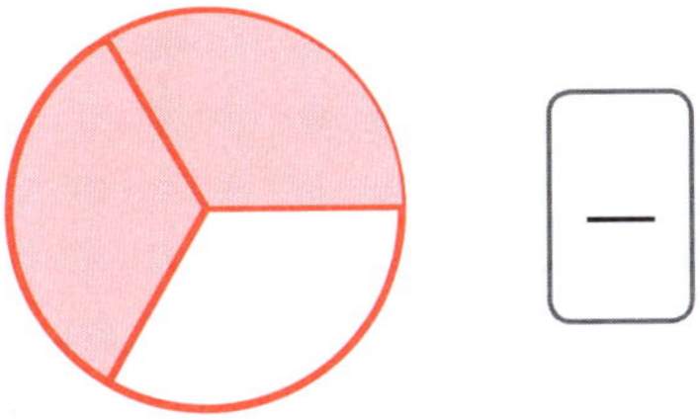

6. 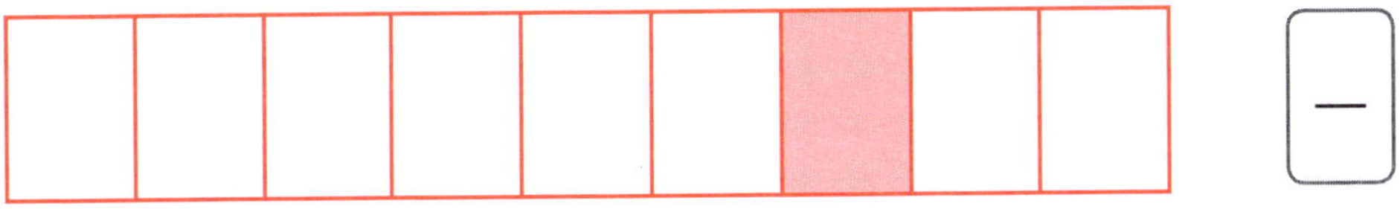

7 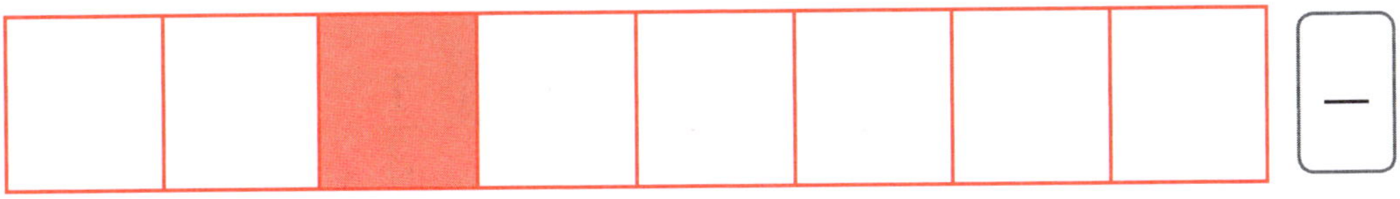

8 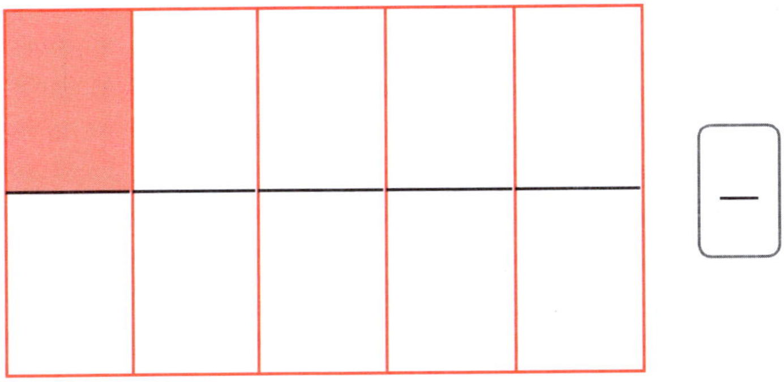

Date.................. Remarks.................... Signature....................

PRACTICE TEST - 1

A. Write the missing numbers:

1.

1	2		4		6		8
	10		12				

2.

25				29			
		35				39	

3.

65			68			71	
	74			77			

4.

52					57		
		62				66	

5.

			81				85
	87			90			

Date.................. Remarks.................... Signature....................

B. Write these numbers in their correct order:

11	17	20	15	18	16	12	14	13	19
11	12	13	14	15	16	17	18	19	20

1. 23 25 30 29 28 24 26 21 27 22

2. 31 34 28 30 32 35 37 29 33 36

3. 74 79 77 81 76 73 82 75 78 80

4. 58 64 55 57 63 56 59 60 62 61

5. 49 48 44 45 43 51 42 46 50 47

6. 25 32 33 27 26 24 28 29 31 30

Date.................... Remarks..................... Signature.....................

C. Rearrange numbers in order:

156	135	98	71	320	223
71	98	135	156	223	320

1.

261	88	249	355	113	174

2.

323	204	181	78	198	313

3.

149	141	239	158	256	130

4.

229	329	128	98	48	292

5.

71	199	319	250	59	200

6.

289	388	138	381	275	251

Date.................. Remarks.................... Signature....................

PRACTICE TEST - 2

A. Write the correct missing number in the stars:

	171	172	173	174	175	176	177
1.		112			115		
2.	165			168		170	
3.			85		87		
4.	29			32			35

B. Write the backward counting:

1.	155					150			
2.	121		119				115		

Date.................... Remarks..................... Signature.....................

3.

177				173		171		

4.

200		198			195			

C. Write in order. Start from the smallest one:

1.

128	126	123	125	129	122

2.

187	182	189	184	183	181

3.

97	96	95	94	93	92

4.

238	235	239	233	231	234

5.

124	129	123	125	122	127

6.

100	93	97	95	91	98

Date.................. Remarks.................... Signature....................

D. Write the biggest and smallest number:

							Biggest	Smallest
1.	99	39	47	110	24	=	______	______
2.	188	124	245	386	290	=	______	______
3.	256	395	289	478	498	=	______	______
4.	123	214	229	156	114	=	______	______
5.	481	389	489	379	478	=	______	______

E. Write the pattern in the blanks:

	134	143	133	211	220	=	133	134
1.	428	441	444	443	240	=		
2.	302	365	356	301	340	=		
3.	154	145	151	165	164	=		
4.	298	241	295	290	299	=		
5.	231	315	319	314	232	=		

Date.................. Remarks.................... Signature....................

PRACTICE TEST - 3

A. Check the arrow and do the following sums:

1.

2.

3.

4.

5.

6.

Date.................. Remarks.................... Signature....................

7.

8.

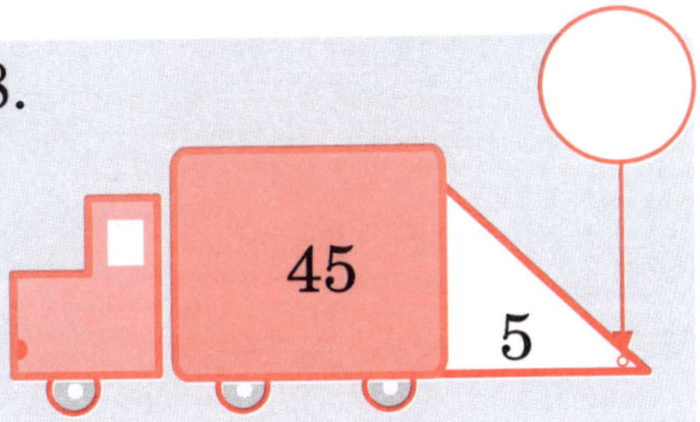

9.

10.

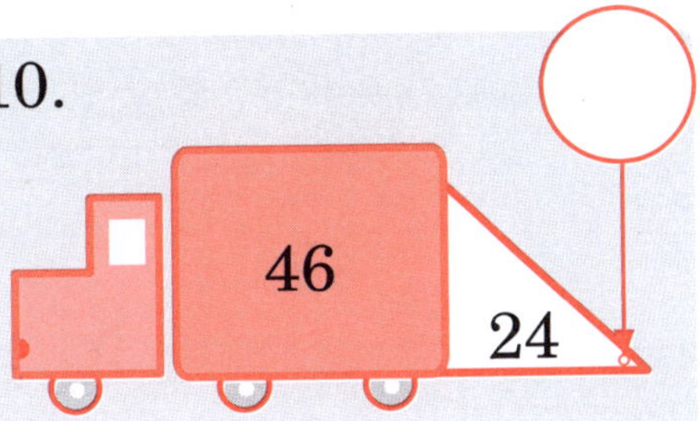

B. Do more:

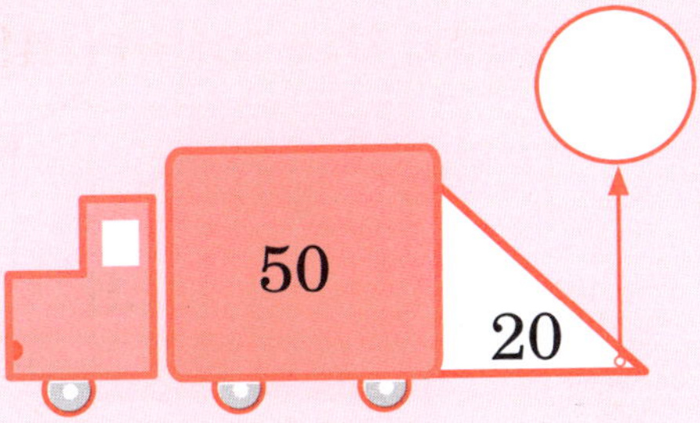

1.

2.

3.

4.

Date.................... Remarks..................... Signature.....................

5.

6.

7.

8.

C. Check the pattern and complete the following:

1.

2.

3.

4.

Date.................... Remarks...................... Signature......................

5.

6.

7.

8.

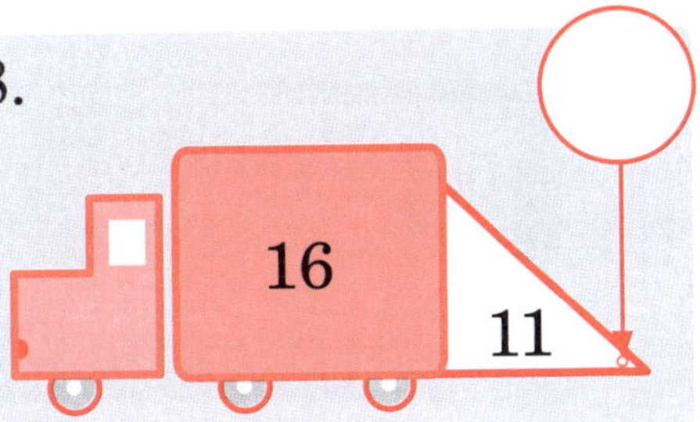

9.

10.

11.

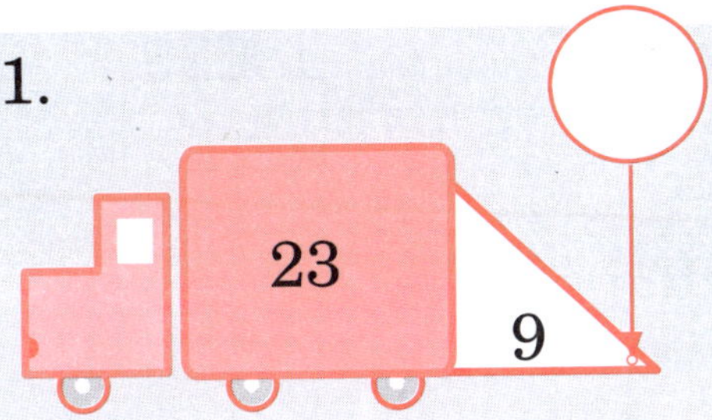

12.

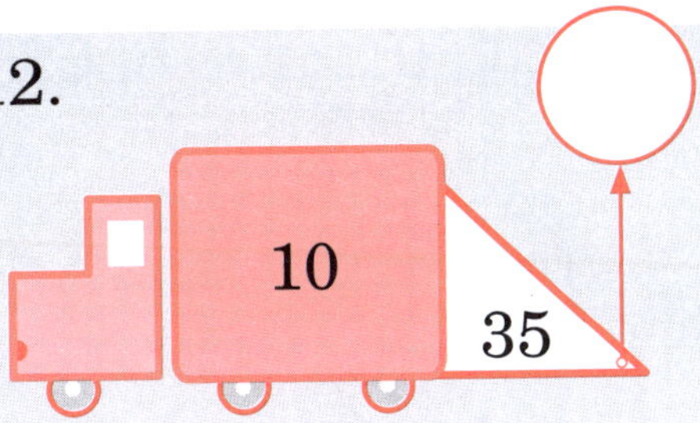

13.

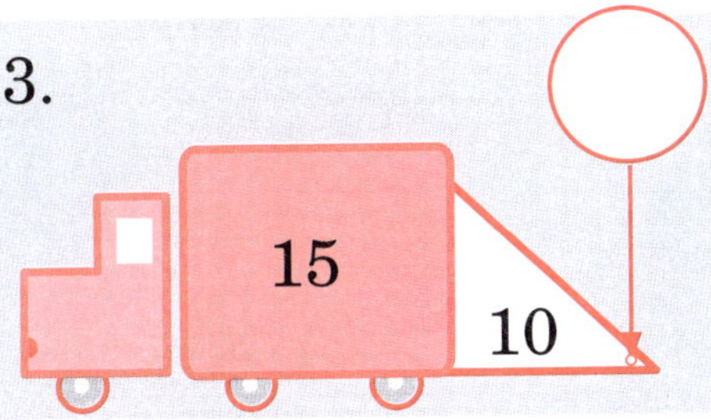

14.

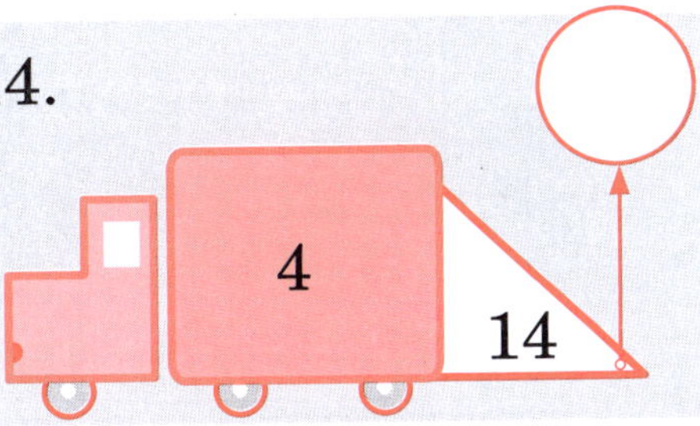

PRACTICE TEST - 4

A. Count the coins and tick (✓) the correct options:

1. 5 + 2 + 10

a. ₵14 b. ₵13 c. ₵17 d. ₵15

2. 5 + 1 + 2

a. ₵10 b. ₵3 c. ₵8 d. ₵5

3. 10 + 5 + 10

a. ₵30 b. ₵25 c. ₵27 d. ₵26

4. 10 + 10 + 10

a. ₵40 b. ₵50 c. ₵30 d. ₵65

5. 10 + 2 + 25

a. ₵40 b. ₵50 c. ₵60 d. ₵37

Date.................... Remarks..................... Signature.....................

6.

a ₵50 b ₵30 c ₵60 d. ₵35

7.

a. ₵40 b. ₵30 c. ₵50 d. ₵35

8.

a. ₵40 b. ₵30 c. ₵57 d. ₵35

9.

a. ₵18 b. ₵16 c. ₵17 d. ₵15

10.

a. ₵100 b. ₵80 c. ₵120 d. ₵90

11.

a. ₵20 b. ₵25 c. ₵15 d. ₵30

12.

a. ₵45 b. ₵50 c. ₵60 d. ₵55

Date.................. Remarks.................... Signature....................

B. Do the following:

1. Hassan has ₵6

He gave ₵1 for 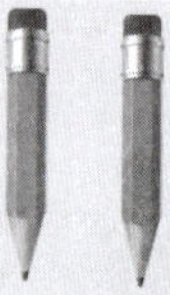

How much change does he get?

2. Sam has ₵15

He gave ₵10 for 

How much change does he get?

3. Zadie has ₵25

She gave ₵15 for 

How much change does he get?

4. Henry has ₵10

He gave ₵5 for 

How much change does he get?

Date.................... Remarks..................... Signature.....................

PRACTICE TEST - 5

A. Write the numbers:

1. fifty = ☐
2. twenty-eight = ☐
3. thirty-four = ☐
4. forty-two = ☐
5. eleven = ☐
6. twenty-nine = ☐
7. forty-eight = ☐
8. twenty-seven = ☐
9. thirty-eight = ☐
10. forty-six = ☐

B. Write the number names:

1. 27= ____________________
2. 16= ____________________
3. 23= ____________________
4. 49= ____________________
5. 33= ____________________
6. 50= ____________________
7. 15= ____________________
8. 19= ____________________
9. 14= ____________________
10. 12= ____________________
11. 41= ____________________
12. 38= ____________________

Date.................. Remarks.................... Signature....................

C. Solve the code:

g	y	s	w	l	h	i	o	e	f	t	r	u	n	v	x
1	2	3	4	5	6	7	8	9	10	11	12	13	14	15	16

eight = 9 7 1 6 11

twelve = 11 4 9 5 15 9

1. nine = ___ ___ ___ ___
2. sixteen = ___ ___ ___ ___ ___ ___ ___
3. twenty = ___ ___ ___ ___ ___ ___
4. eighteen = ___ ___ ___ ___ ___ ___ ___ ___
5. eleven = ___ ___ ___ ___ ___ ___
6. twenty four = ___ ___ ___ ___ ___ ___ ___ ___ ___ ___
7. fifteen = ___ ___ ___ ___ ___ ___ ___
8. forty = ___ ___ ___ ___ ___
9. ten = ___ ___ ___
10. fourteen = ___ ___ ___ ___ ___ ___ ___ ___

Date.................. Remarks.................... Signature....................

PRACTICE TEST - 6

A. Fill in the blanks:

1. 3 x 3 = ☐
2. 2 x 3 = ☐
3. 4 x 8 = ☐
4. 2 x 4 = ☐
5. 3 x 5 = ☐
6. 4 x 5 = ☐
7. 5 x 10 = ☐
8. 2 x 9 = ☐
9. 5 x 7 = ☐
10. 3 x 9 = ☐
11. 4 x 10 = ☐
12. 5 x 5 = ☐
13. 3 x 10 = ☐
14. 5 x 6 = ☐
15. 2 x 10 = ☐
16. 5 x 4 = ☐
17. 4 x 4 = ☐
18. 2 x 8 = ☐
19. 3 x 7 = ☐
20. 4 x 3 = ☐
21. 5 x 9 = ☐
22. 2 x 7 = ☐
23. 4 x 6 = ☐
24. 3 x 8 = ☐
25. 2 x 6 = ☐
26. 3 x 6 = ☐
27. 4 x 9 = ☐
28. 5 x 2 = ☐
29. 4 x 7 = ☐
30. 5 x 3 = ☐

Date.................. Remarks.................... Signature....................

B. Complete the tables-2, 3, 4, and 5:

1.

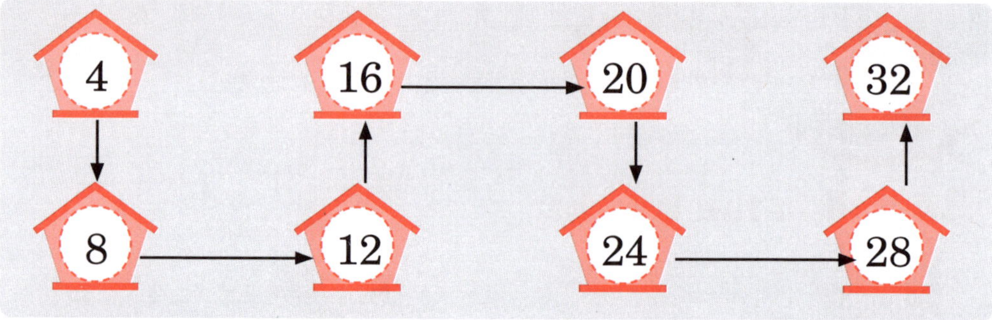

2.

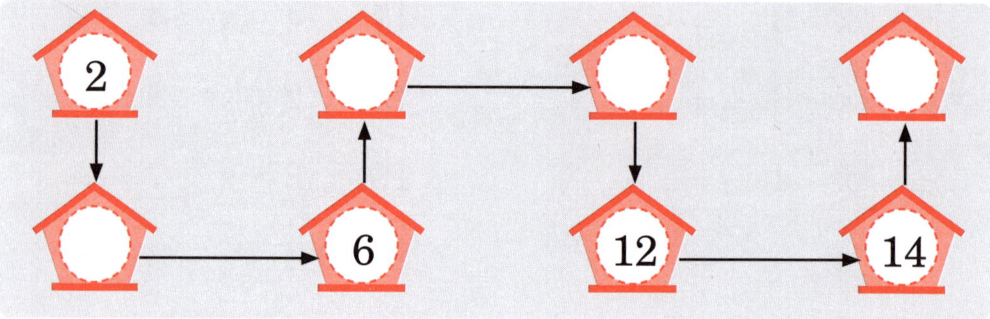

3.

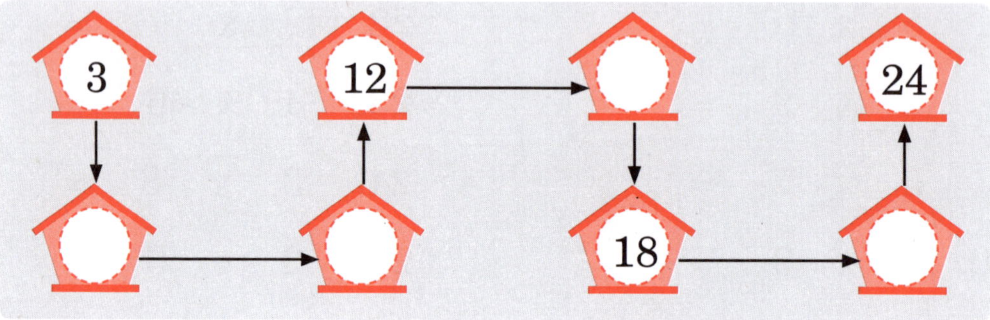

4.

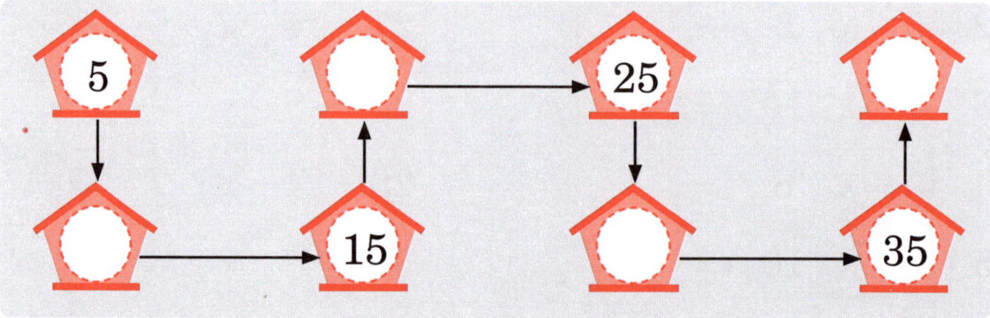

Date.................. Remarks.................... Signature....................

5.

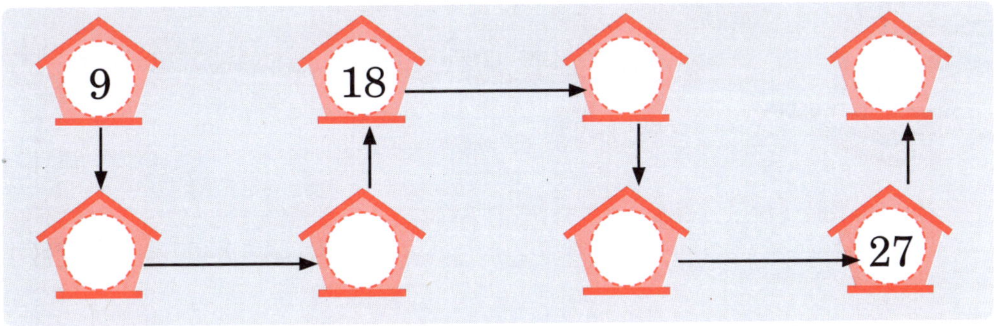

6.

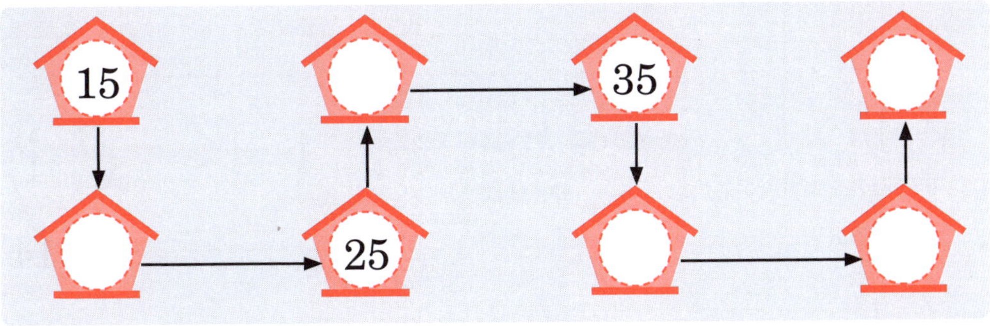

7.

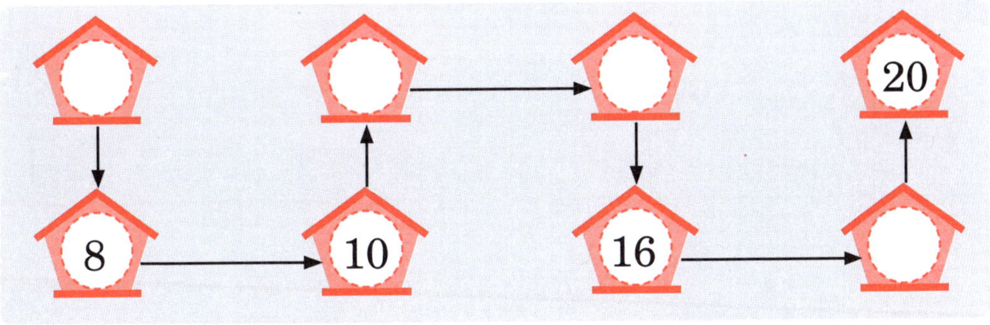

8.

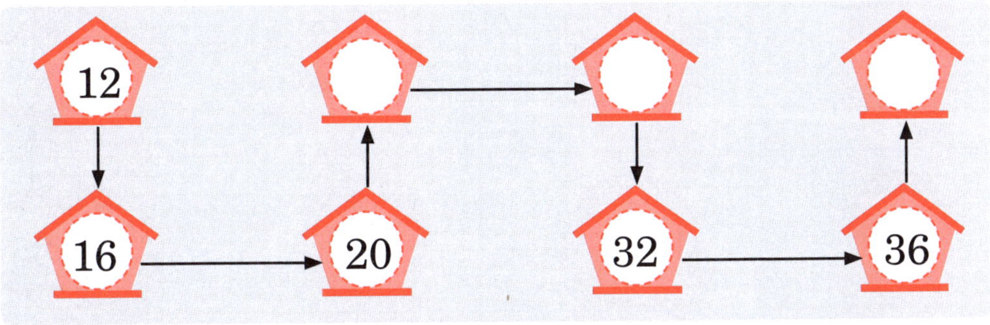

Date.................... Remarks..................... Signature.....................

PRACTICE TEST - 7

A. Tick (✓) the similar shape and colour them:

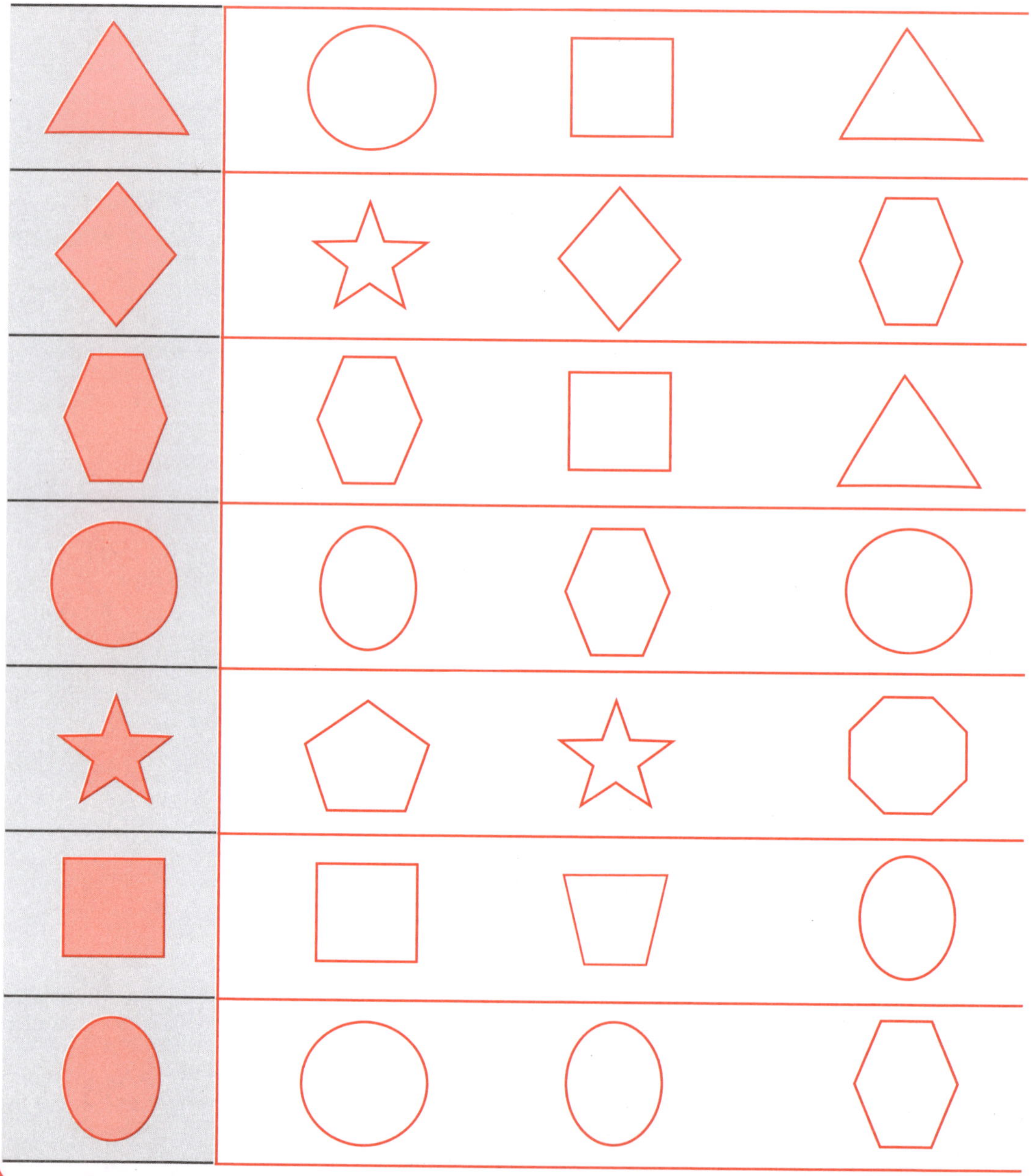

Date.................. Remarks.................... Signature....................

B. Divide these shapes into half and colour one half of each shape:

Date.................. Remarks.................... Signature....................

PRACTICE TEST - 8

A. Tick (✓) the correct answer and fill in the blanks:

1. A square has __________ sides.
   (a) three (b) four

2. A triangle has __________sides.
   (a) two (b) three

3. A circle has ____________line.
   (a) curved (b) slanting

4. An oval looks like an ________
   (a) orange (b) egg

5. A rectangle has _________big sides.
   (a) four (b) two

B. Match the following pictures with their shapes:

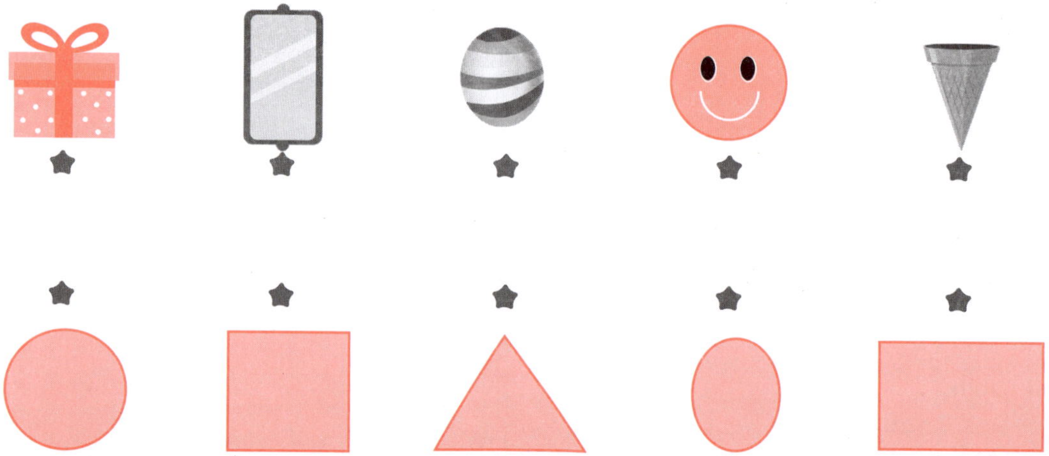

Date.................. Remarks.................... Signature....................

C. Name the shaded fractions:

1.

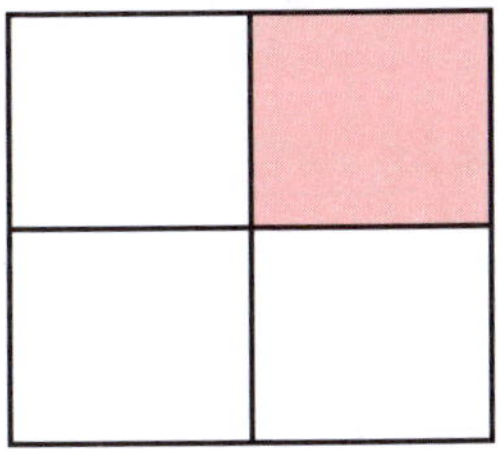

$\frac{1}{4}$

2.

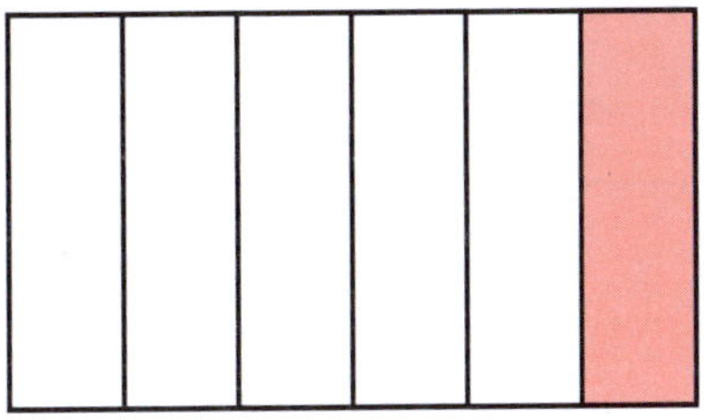

3.

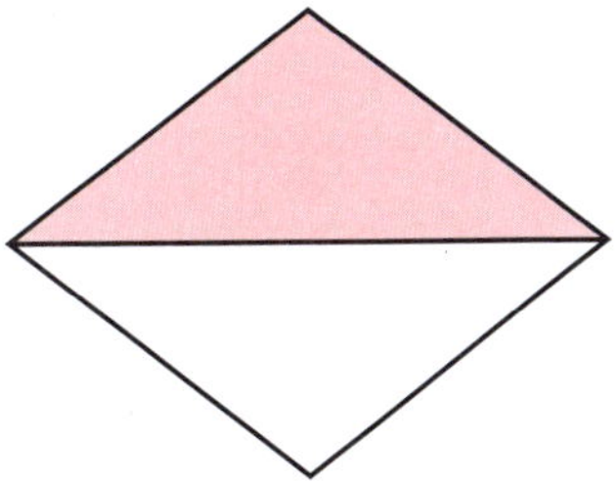

4.

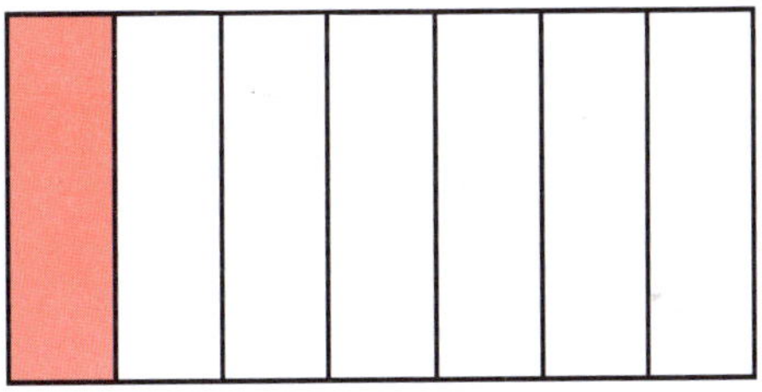

5.

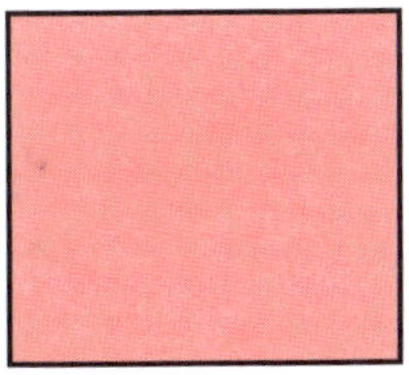

6.

Date.................. Remarks.................... Signature....................

7.

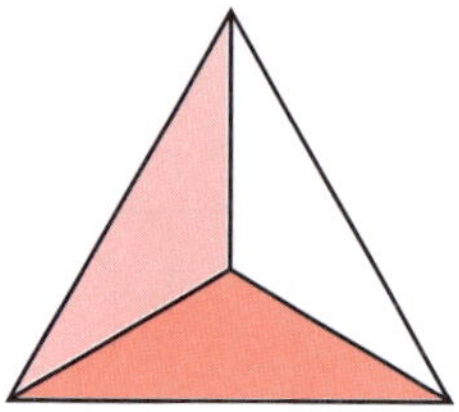

8.

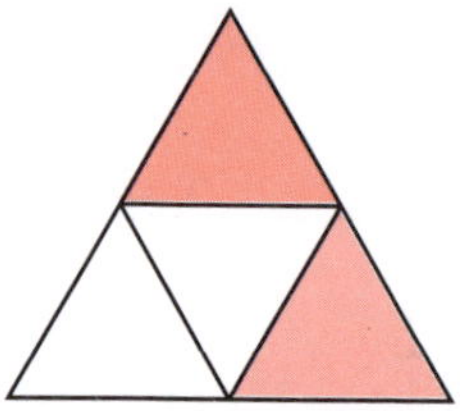

9.

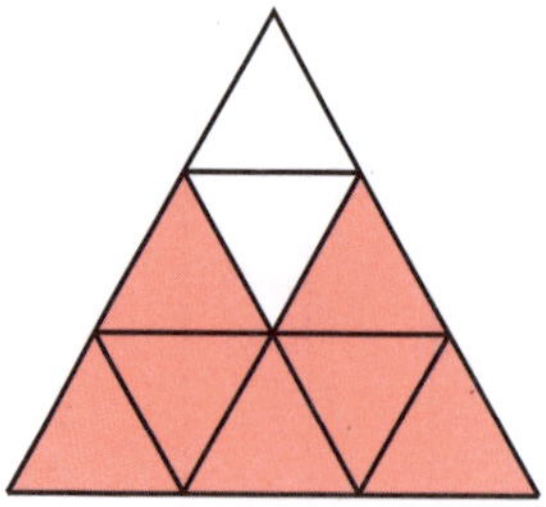

10.

11.

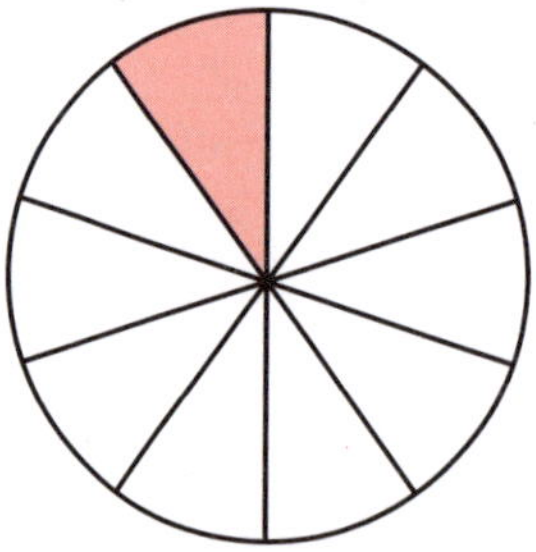

12.

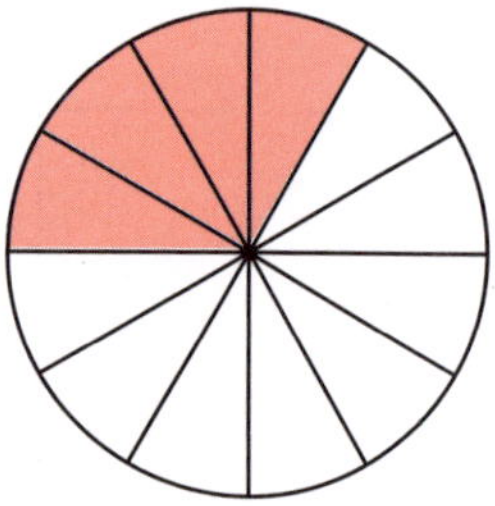

Date.................... Remarks...................... Signature......................